Showing Gratitude
Life's Outtakes - Year 18

52 Humorous and Inspirational Short Stories

By
Daris Howard

A collection of stories, humorous anecdotes, thoughts, and tidbits of wisdom from the newspaper column *Life's Outtakes*.

Publishing Inspiration

Showing Gratitude

Life's Outtakes - Year 18

52 Humorous and Inspirational Short Stories

By

Daris W. Howard

A collection of stories, humorous anecdotes, thoughts, and tidbits of wisdom from the newspaper column *Life's Outtakes*.

ISBN-10: 1-62986-037-9
ISBN-13: 978-1-62986-037-4

www.publishinginspiration.com

Publishing Date: May 9, 2025

Publishing Inspiration LLC

Table of Contents

Dear Reader,

People often ask me if my stories are true. Though I admit that I tend to take a bit of literary license in my writing, each story is based on an actual event. Sometimes the stranger stories are the ones that are stretched the least. As people often say, truth is stranger than fiction.

I also want to note that some of the names have been changed to protect the anonymity of the individuals.

Daris Howard

Bob

My mom loved to tell the story of her dog, Bob. Mom was not much of one for pets. She grew up during the Depression, and to stay around the farm, animals had to have some productive value, such as giving milk or eggs. Cats at her home ran wild, catching their own food. If they were good at that, they were allowed a home in the barn, but nothing more. The only other animals were cattle, horses, and chickens. Anything else was another mouth to feed and was unneeded and unwanted.

But one day, when Mom was about five, a stray dog wandered into the yard. It was haggard, ragged, and extremely timid. It obviously hadn't eaten in a while, and his mangy fur showed that he likely belonged to no one. Mom's parents said he could stay for one good meal, then he needed to find another home. They offered a good meal to all the people traveling through looking for work but could share little more. They felt they should do the same for the dog.

They gave the dog some scraps of food they found and a little milk. He ate it like he hadn't eaten in years. Mom wanted to brush him before sending him on his way, but her parents forbade it. They were afraid she might get too attached.

After the dog had eaten, Mom's father shooed it up the driveway and back to the road it had come from.

Mom decided to walk out to her brothers who were working to get the hay in. She decided to cut across the cow pasture. She had been told never to go in there because the bull could be unpredictable, but it was a shorter distance, and the bull, along with the cows, were at the far end of the pasture. But when she reached the middle of the pasture, the bull saw her and was apparently in a bad mood. He came at her from about a hundred yards away.

Her parents and brothers heard her screams but were too far away to reach her in time. But the stray dog wasn't. He had returned and wandered out with her, though he kept his distance, shying away from all humans.

As the bull charged, Mom's brothers and parents ran to her aid, but the bull was far closer and running much faster. Mom's family members screamed and waved their arms as they ran, trying to draw the bull's attention. But nothing could distract him from his target; at least, nothing could until a small dog suddenly appeared in his path and started barking and growling ferociously.

The bull slid to a stop, and he and the dog had a standoff. They circled each other, and then the bull rushed the dog. The dog leapt out of the way at the last instant like an expert bullfighter, then he jumped and sank his teeth into the bull's fleshy skin on his hip. The bull bellowed in pain and spun to free himself from the dog. The dog was flung a short distance; then the two faced off again. Once again, the bull charged with the same results. This happened a few more times before the bull finally decided he had had enough. He ran back to the herd to cry to the cows about his cruel mistreatment.

As the rest of the family arrived, the dog fearfully started to slink away.

My mom's father said, "Joyce, call the dog to you. He seems to have some affection for you."

My mom called the dog. He stopped, but didn't come to her. The others had to back away before he would, but he did come after the others gave her some space.

"Can I pet him, Daddy?" she asked.

Her father nodded. "Why not? I think he feels he's your dog."

They named him Bob because he had a bobbed tail. And that's how the farm got another animal.

"After all," Mom's dad said, "saving a family member is probably the most productive thing an animal can do."

(To be continued)

2

A Smart Dog

After the stray dog saved Joyce's life, it was allowed to stay, and Bob quickly became part of the family. The first thing Joyce did was give him a bath and a good brushing. When she finished, her brothers, Mathol and Delos, gathered around.

Mathol petted Bob and said, "He's a right nice-looking animal when he's clean."

"True," Delos said. "He doesn't even look like the same animal."

But the cleaning showed something else strange about Bob. He had an unusual number of scars. "Daddy," Joyce asked her father, "what do you think all of those scars are from?"

Her father shook his head. "There's something familiar about them, but I can't think what it is."

Bob spent a lot of time with Joyce. He was timid around everyone else, but he didn't seem afraid of her since she was only five. But he soon took his part in other ways around the farm. When Delos and Mathol headed to the pasture to get the cows for milking, Bob liked to go along. Delos and Mathol enjoyed his company, too.

After Bob had saved Joyce from the bull, the bull was more humble. But the bull still challenged Bob a couple more times. Bob was so expert at dodging the bull, and then sinking his teeth into the bull's soft backside, that two more challenges were all the bull was good for. After that, when he saw that the boys had Bob with them, the bull ran to the farthest end of the pasture and let the cows fend for themselves.

Twice each day, the boys drove the cows to the barn for milking, and Bob hurried up the stragglers. But one day, a cow tried to break free. Delos yelled for Mathol to cut her off. Mathol barely headed her in time and turned her back to the pen. As soon as she was in, Mathol shut the gate and latched it.

A couple of days later, the same cow tried to make a break for it. But neither of the boys was near enough to stop her. However, Bob soon had her turned around and drove her back to the pen. But then he did something unexpected. He pushed the gate shut with his nose, then he used his teeth to pull the latch closed. The two boys stood there, dumbfounded. Finally, Mathol turned to Delos. "Did you see what I just saw, or was I dreaming?"

"Yeah, I saw it," Delos said. "Bob is better at herding cows than you are. But that's not such a big miracle. Everyone is."

"Ha, ha, ha," Mathol said. "Why don't you push the gate closed with your nose then use your teeth to shut the latch?"

That night they told the rest of the family what had happened, and the others were skeptical. Later, when they were milking again, Delos mentioned the family's uncertainty about what they shared.

"Well, it might be because you have a way of building on stories until they aren't even recognizable," Mathol said.

"A story shouldn't be told more than once if you can't tell it better each time," Delos replied.

They wondered to each other if Bob would do his trick again. "Let's try next time," Mathol said. So, when it was time to get the cows, they went to the pasture. Bob followed them as usual, but this time, Mathol pointed at the cows and said, "Bob, go get the cows."

It took a couple of times saying it, but suddenly Bob took off toward the cows. He rounded them up and brought them back to the milking pen.

"Let's see what he does with the gate," Delos said.

Once the cows were in the pen, Bob pushed the gate shut and latched it. After Bob had done this twice each day for a week, the boys called the rest of the family to watch.

Their father shook his head in disbelief. "I've never seen anything like it. Let's just hope the cows don't learn his gate tricks."

(To be continued)

4

Freeing Bob the Dog

Bob, the dog, had really become part of the family, saving five-year-old Joyce from the bull and showing that he could bring the cows from the pasture for milking, even closing and latching the gate. Sometimes the family members wondered how he had learned to do everything he did. Then, one day, they got an inkling.

Joyce was brushing Bob after a bath. The brushing he liked, the bath not so much. She was still trying to get the burrs out of his fur when a pickup pulled into the yard.

Gas was hard to pay for during the depression, so when any vehicle came, it caused great curiosity. Arden, Joyce's father, went to meet the visitors. Though they were quite a distance away, Joyce could hear the conversation. The man said he was from the circus, and they had just arrived in town. He needed some hay for some animals and had heard word that Arden had some he might sell.

Cash was in short supply, so Arden was happy to sell what they could spare from feeding their own animals. He invited the man to the house. As they approached, suddenly Bob jumped to his feet and started barking. He moved into attack position and bared his teeth.

The man stopped. His face deepened into an angry scowl. "Shadow, you stupid mutt. How did you get clear out here from Chicago?"

"Shadow?" Arden asked.

"Yes," the man said. "That is my dog. I trained him to do all sorts of tricks." The man then turned to Bob and commanded, "Shadow, lie down."

But Bob didn't lie down. If anything, his growl became lower and more threatening. The man pulled a whip from a loop on his belt. "I'll teach you to growl at me."

But as he brought the whip back to strike, Arden grabbed the man's wrist. "If you touch that dog with a whip, I'll use it on you."

The man jerked his wrist from Arden's grasp. "That is my dog, and I will have him back."

"That dog is not leaving this farm," Arden said.

"We'll see," the man said. He then went to his truck and left.

"Daddy, you aren't going to let that mean man take Bob, are you?" Joyce asked.

"No," Arden said. "He is part of the family."

Bob had barely calmed down when the man returned with the sheriff following close behind. After they had both exited their vehicles, the man pointed at Bob, who bristled again. "That is my dog, and I demand to have him returned."

"Can you prove it?" the sheriff asked.

"I have lots of papers," the man said.

"Papers mean nothing," Arden said. "If a dog belongs to a man, he should be able to call and have him come."

"That's true," the sheriff said to the man. "Why don't you call him?"

The man took a deep breath, turned to Bob, and commanded, "Here, Shadow."

Bob bared his teeth, got into an attack stance, and growled.

"But I can show you markings that will verify he is my dog," the man said.

"Like the whip marks all over him?" Arden asked. "I knew they were familiar. I recognize them from the dogs and horses we worked with in the Great War. Some men mishandled them."

"Well," the sheriff said, "I am not inclined to believe you have proven he is yours."

"Look," Arden said. "I am an honest man. Even if he is yours, as you claim, maybe we can trade some hay for the dog. You wanted four wagon loads. How about we give you one for free for the dog?"

"How about three?" the man said.

"You haven't even proven he is yours," Arden replied. "I can't go higher than two."

"Okay," the man said. "Two it will be, and you can keep the ungrateful mutt."

When the wagons arrived to pick up the hay, Arden's wife was concerned. "Can we spare two loads of hay to them for free?"

Arden smiled. "We'll be okay, and it is a small price to pay to free Bob from the life he has had."

(To be continued)

It's Not About Being Perfect

Bob had saved Joyce's life when she was only five, so her father had let him stay on the farm. Bob showed he was an intelligent dog, even capable of getting the cows in for milking and shutting the gate by himself. Joyce thought Bob was almost human. But one day, as she and Bob were walking through the pasture, something happened to remind her that he still had the instincts of a dog.

They started crossing a canal that ran through the pasture. Lying across the canal was a fallen tree that was about two feet in diameter. Bob was behind her as they crossed. Suddenly, a rabbit ran out of the brush on the far side of the canal.

Bob darted past Joyce on his way to chase the rabbit, but in so doing, he knocked her off balance. Joyce slipped and plunged into the icy cold water. She was only seven and could not swim. As she surfaced and gasped for air, there was a splash beside her, and Bob was there.

As Joyce struggled to keep her head above water, Bob grabbed her shirt with his teeth and swam hard for shore. But the water was swift and deep. It was pulling them toward the check where a headgate split the water into two directions. Water checks on the canal often had a dangerous undertow.

Bob fought the water desperately, trying to get them to the only place between where they were and the check that someone could find a way out of the water. Seeing what he was doing, Joyce started kicking her feet to move them in that direction. It seemed like forever as they fought their way across the current, and just as Joyce was afraid the current would pull past their hopeful landing spot, she was able to grab a branch and pull herself to safety.

But Bob was too tired and could not save himself, and he floated toward the check. Suddenly, a big, strong hand reached over the cement wall leading into the check, grabbed Bob by his fur, and pulled him onto the bank to safety. Joyce looked up to see that it was her father.

Bob had swallowed lots of water and had lost consciousness. Joyce's father started pumping the dog's chest, and some water came out of Bob's lungs. Suddenly, Bob gulped a deep breath. He sputtered air and coughed up more water, but he started to breathe. Soon, he opened his eyes.

Joyce hugged her dog, happy that he was going to be okay. But when she looked at her father, she could tell he was not happy.

"Joyce, how did you end up in the canal?" he asked.

Joyce was afraid that if she told him Bob had caused her to slip, her father would be angry with the dog and make him leave. She took a deep breath and said, "I was crossing the tree and slipped."

"I have told you repeatedly to stay away from the canal," he replied. "If I can't trust you to do that, I must insist you stay at the house."

Joyce loved her freedom to roam, but as much as he hated the punishment, she felt equally bad knowing she had not told her father the whole truth because of her concern about what he would think of Bob.

However, later that evening, she decided she had to tell her father the whole story. After she did, she said, "Daddy, even though Bob made me fall in the canal, you won't make him leave, will you?"

Her father pulled her onto his lap. "Joyce, everyone makes mistakes. You did in disobeying me. Bob did in letting his instincts to go after a rabbit caused him to make you slip. But the critical thing is that when a person, or a dog, makes a mistake, they need to do their best to fix it. You made a mistake in not telling me the whole truth, and you are trying to fix it. Bob also fixed his error by forgetting the rabbit and diving in to save you. I will definitely not send Bob away. Today, he showed how incredible he is by saving you, even at the possible cost of his life."

Joyce's father then smiled. "And your punishment still holds. You can't leave the area around the house for a week."

Joyce nodded. She had learned a valuable lesson, and her bond with her dog had grown even stronger.

(Continued)

Making the Way Home

Joyce's dog, Bob, had been with the family for six years. From the time he saved Joyce's life when she was five, he had become an integral family member. But one morning, right after they had finished harvest, Joyce called for Bob, but he never came.

She had never had that happen before. Sometimes, he might take a few minutes getting there. He might be far out in the pasture or finishing getting the cows in for milking, but he always came. She called many times. She went to all his favorite places and the ones they liked to visit together.

The last spot she checked was under the old apple tree. She and Bob spent hours there. Once she learned to read, she would read stories to him. He would lie with his head in her lap, and she would gently stroke his fur as she read.

But he was at none of these spots. Joyce went to find her father. He called the family together, and they made an exhaustive search Her brothers even rode horses to ask the neighbors, but no one had seen Bob.

Joyce was heartbroken. "He wouldn't just leave."

"Maybe he decided his job was done here," her father said. "Perhaps he decided it was time to move on. After all, he just wandered in here when he came."

Joyce shook her head. "That doesn't sound like Bob."

It wasn't until later that she learned her father assumed coyotes had killed Bob, as they had many other dogs in the area. But he said what he did because he felt it would be more comforting.

For a couple of weeks, Joyce went out every morning and called for Bob, hoping beyond hope that he had come home. But finally, she quit, sure he would never return.

Then, almost a month after he disappeared, the family was eating breakfast when they heard a scratch at the back door and a whimper. Joyce almost knocked her food to the floor in her haste to get to the door. She opened it, and there lay Bob. He was emaciated, could hardly move, and was covered with blood. Joyce hugged him. Her father patted her to have her move aside, then he gently took Bob in his arms and carried him inside. Joyce's mother got an old blanket and made a bed by the fireplace.

Joyce got Bob some milk and warmed it at her mother's suggestion. The temperature outside was below freezing, and Bob was shivering, though he didn't seem to have the energy even to do that. When Joyce gave him the milk, he tried to stand to drink but couldn't. Her mother got a cloth, soaked it in milk, then drizzled it into Bob's mouth. Joyce saw how and soon took over Bob's feeding.

Joyce's father checked Bob for wounds and found that the blood was coming from his blistered and lacerated feet. They were cleaned and bandaged. It was days before anyone was sure Bob would live, and more than a week before he could stand. But within a month, he was again running with Joyce up the lane to the mailbox.

The next fall, when the immigrant crew that helped with the harvest came, Bob suddenly blocked their path, growling and baring his teeth at them. The men started backing away as Bob approached, looking like he would attack. Joyce's father called Bob back.

The men seemed confused and were babbling in their language. Luckily, one of Joyce's brothers understood them. The family learned that the men had admired Bob's ability with cattle and had stolen him the last fall. They had taken him nearly 2,000 miles away to their next harvest area. Bob left the minute they let him go.

Once the harvest crew's leader realized the family knew what they had done, he begged forgiveness and asked that they still be allowed to work. Joyce's father was angry, but the family needed the help. However, they kept an eye on everything, and Bob slept in the house at night.

Joyce considered the distance and the time Bob was gone, and she realized Bob must have traveled over seventy miles a day.

But he did it to make his way home—his home and his family, and that made her love him even more.

Losing a Friend

    Joyce had had her dog Bob since she was five. But it seemed like he had always been there. He was one of her best friends. When kids at school were mean, she could always come home and find Bob waiting for her.

    She was now sixteen, and her older brothers were off fighting in the war. She missed them. She now had a younger brother and sister, and that helped, but many things fell to her since she was the oldest child at home, even things that men usually did. Without her brothers, her father needed her help even more.

    They did hire some German soldiers from a prison camp in the area. The prisoners liked to work at the farm because Joyce's family fed them well, and food at the camp was rationed. But the one constant in all of it was Bob. When the turmoil of life became overwhelming, in the evening, after chores were done, Joyce would still take Bob and read under the apple tree.

    But that year when she turned sixteen, Joyce started noticing a change in Bob. His whiskers turned gray, and he did everything more slowly. He was still there to meet her after school, but he walked slower going home.

    Joyce's father noticed as well. He told Joyce and her siblings to stop sending Bob to get the cows in for milking. Whenever the bull had attacked Bob, Bob had expertly dodged the bull, then given the bull a sharp bite for the trouble. But Bob's reflexes weren't what they had been, and Joyce's father was afraid that if the bull ever attacked again, Bob would be hurt.

    As time went on, Bob struggled to keep up with Joyce, even on the most casual walk. But she knew the end was getting close the morning she called for Bob and he didn't come. That had only happened once before, and that was when the migrant workers had stolen him. But this time she went to find him, and he was still lying in his bed.

He tried to rise to greet her, but his legs trembled, and he fell back into the straw. Joyce ran to get her father.

He checked Bob over and said, "He's suffering a lot. Maybe we should put him down."

It was not the way of farm life to let an animal suffer, but Joyce couldn't stand the thought of having Bob's time on earth ended by them. She pleaded with her father not to.

Her father sighed. "I can understand how you feel, Joyce. But you can see in his eyes that he is hurting."

Tears flowed down Joyce's face. "Please, Father. I will do what I can to make him comfortable."

Her father nodded and left to take care of the chores.

Joyce kept her promise. She changed the straw on Bob's bed every day. She made sure he had good milk to drink because he couldn't eat anything else. As Bob's condition deteriorated further and he couldn't even sit up enough to lap the milk, Joyce would soak a rag and squeeze the milk out into Bob's mouth as she had done when he was sick once before.

But one night, Bob wouldn't even take that milk, and Joyce knew it was the end. She sat down in the straw, pulled Bob's head onto her lap, and lovingly stroked his fur. When she finally had to go to bed, using all the strength he had, Bob raised his head and licked her face. The next morning, he was gone.

Joyce's father asked her where she wanted to bury Bob, and she chose a beautiful spot by the apple tree. She and her father took turns digging the grave while the younger children and Joyce's mother looked on. When they finished burying him, Joyce fell to her knees and sobbed.

Her father pulled her into his arms, and even though most teenagers held back at such things, she was grateful for his strength. She looked into his face and asked, "Father, do you think all dogs go to heaven?"

He smiled kindly. "There are a few I've known I have my doubts about, but I know one I am sure is there now."

Joyce smiled. She was sure of it, too.

Welcome Home

(Conclusion of Bob the Dog)

My mother was 96 and living in an assisted living center. Her heart was struggling, and she was having a hard time getting enough oxygen. She had gone into hospice care but often refused their help. I was on call in case they needed me for anything.

One morning, they rang and asked me to come down. I immediately left work and drove over. When I walked in, the nurse was suggesting some morphine to help Mom, but Mom was leery about it, as she seemed to be about most things at that point in her life.

"Joyce, it will help you relax and get more oxygen," the nurse said.

"I don't trust it or the doctor that prescribed it," Mom said.

The nurse noticed me and asked me to convince Mom to take it. I shook my head. Even though I had power given to me to make decisions for her, I refused to go against her wishes.

"Is there anything else, maybe something milder, that you could give her?" I asked.

The nurse sighed. "Yes, but it is slow-acting and will take a half hour or more to have any real effect. She is so tense and combative because of lack of oxygen."

I talked to Mom, and she agreed to take the milder medicine. The nurse nodded and gave it to her. Then she said, "Maybe you can find a way to calm her down. That will help her more than about anything."

Mom knew she wasn't doing well, so after the nurse left, she said, "Son, you've read a lot about what happens after a person dies. What will it be like?"

"From what I've read, those you love come to meet you."

"Do you think your dad will be there?" she asked.

"Of course," I replied.

"How about your brothers?"

I answered in the affirmative. Then she started naming others she hoped would meet her. There were her parents, her siblings, and some grandparents. As she talked about them, her tension appeared to melt away, and her breathing stabilized. She then started mentioning friends. Being 96, most of her friends were already gone, but she couldn't remember names and grew anxious again. I named a few, but it didn't help much. Then I thought of something.

"Mom, how about Bob?"

Mom spoke with a disgusted tone. "I don't know anyone named Bob."

"I'm talking about Bob, your dog."

It took a moment, but suddenly she smiled. "Old Bob."

She then turned to me and said, "Have I told you about the time he accidentally knocked me into the canal, then he nearly died himself saving me?"

Though I had heard the story many times, I simply said, "Tell me, Mom."

She told me the story, then told me the one about the migrants stealing Bob and taking him thousands of miles from home, only to have him return. She told quite a few stories about him, then she leaned up on an elbow. "Son, do you really think dogs go to heaven?"

"There are some I have doubts about," I replied. "But I feel what makes it heaven is being with those we love. I don't think it would be heaven without the animals we care about."

Mom smiled. "I don't think so, either." She then rested back on her pillow and said, "I think I'll sleep now."

She closed her eyes and spoke Bob's name once more before her breathing became steady. The nurse came in and gasped. "What did you do?"

"It wasn't me," I said, "It was Bob."

I explained it to her, and she smiled. It wasn't too many days later that Mom left his life. I struggled a lot with my grief. However, when it would become overwhelming, I would think of those who would be there to greet her—Dad, my brothers, her family, and her friends.

But most of all, I would envision a small, bobtailed dog running joyfully to her, happy to welcome his friend home.

Needed on the Team

As math class ended, Aiden's teacher asked him if they could visit. "Sure," Aiden said. "What about?"

"How about we go to my office?" his teacher said.

Besides teaching math, Mr. Hill also taught the science classes, drove the bus, did some janitorial work, was the boys' athletic coach, and was the principal. It was a very small school, and everyone did multiple things. Because of that, when Mr. Hill asked to speak to you, you never knew what it was about.

After they stepped into the principal's office, Mr. Hill motioned Aiden to sit down as he closed the door. Mr. Hill then went around his desk and sat himself across from Aiden.

He looked Aiden in the face and smiled. "Aiden, I looked at the football list for this fall and saw that you didn't put your name on it."

Aiden nodded. "I'd much rather be fishing and hunting than playing football."

"That puts us in a bit of a dilemma," Mr. Hill said. "Having a six-man football team requires six young men and one replacement. Counting you, there are only six young men in the high school who can play."

"But you just said there had to be seven total," Aiden said.

Mr. Hill nodded. "Sam is the seventh. You know he has trouble running and walking because of his cerebral palsy. But he has a brave heart and wants to participate. He will be the water boy, my assistant, and the all-around replacement."

"But how can he be the replacement if he can't really play?" Aiden asked.

"First, we'll hope no one gets hurt," Mr. Hill replied. "If someone does, we've worked it out to put him far behind the line of action. If anyone comes his way, and he can't get out of the road, he knows he is just supposed to drop on the ground. His parents have agreed to it since he wants so badly to be part of the team."

"I don't know," Aiden said. "I was really looking forward to getting a big elk this fall."

"We have had a team almost every year since six-man football was introduced in the nineteen thirties," Mr. Hill said. "We've almost always brought home a trophy."

Aiden smiled. "I understand that in some of those years, many of the teams couldn't get enough players and there were like only two teams in the district competition. Taking second out of two teams is like being a first-place loser. Basically, we couldn't really have done worse."

Mr. Hill laughed. "Being your math teacher, I know your logical mind and should have guessed you'd think of that. But the key thing here, Aiden, is not whether we win or lose. We want to win, obviously, but the other boys want to play, and they won't be able to if you don't. And there is actually one thing less than second out of two teams."

Aiden looked at him skeptically. "And just what is that?"

"Not doing it at all," Mr. Hill answered. "I won't try to pressure you, but I hope you'll think about your friends and also how much this one thing brings our little community together."

Aiden did think a lot about that conversation all evening as he did his chores. His friends had asked him if he was going to sign up, and when he said he was unsure, they didn't pressure him. He had known most of them since first grade, and they were all his friends. They had always had his back when he needed it.

He thought about Sam, who struggled with so many things yet had the courage to be part of the team. He thought lastly about the community. He had never attended a game himself, but he heard plenty about them after each one was played. Maybe it was time for him to be a team player and be there for the other boys and the community.

Having never seen any kind of football game, he wasn't sure what he was in for, but the next morning, when he got to school, Aiden put his name on the team list.

(To be continued)

Teamwork and Dates

    Aiden reluctantly decided to play on his high school's six-man football team because he was one of only six boys in the school that could play. The seventh, Sam, was the water boy, coach's assistant, and all-around replacement, even though he struggled with cerebral palsy. Sam tried to work out some with the others but mostly ended up commanding the whistle that he blew to push the others through their drills.

    Aiden struggled to get his head into the game. All he could think about was the time he was missing hunting. This was to be the year he bagged his first elk. But as time passed, running drills and blocking for each other drew the team together and strengthened friendships in a way all those years together hadn't.

    The week of the first game was also Homecoming. Because some teams ended up canceling due to a lack of players, the first home game that was actually going to be played was always declared as Homecoming. All the other players had dates to the dance, even Sam. But most of the students in the school found dates from somewhere else. Aiden seldom associated with students from other schools, and he couldn't really ask the girls from his own school. They were all like sisters. In fact, one was his sister, and two were his cousins. His possible relation to the others was likely.

    A few days before the game, the players were given uniforms. There were only ten to choose from. They were all threadbare, and some were patched. Even though they had been cleaned, most of them had stains from top to bottom. Sam's uniform was a little loose on him. Almost all the other players had the same problem, except for Jason, the biggest player. His might even have been a bit snug.

    When the other team, the Badgers, showed up, Aiden noted their appearance was similar to his own team: few players and worn-out uniforms. The only exception was they had eight on their team instead of seven.

As Aiden stepped onto the field, he suddenly felt butterflies. He looked at the crowd and estimated there were around seventy people there. It looked like everyone in the town had come, and he hadn't expected that. Aiden looked at the sideline and saw that every girl in the school, except Sarah, was a cheerleader. Sarah thought sports were stupid. The cheerleaders were dressed in their own personal gym shorts, but they all wore matching shirts.

The cheerleaders did a cheer as the team entered. "We are the bears! We are strong! Go against us, and you won't last long!"

As they went out to play, Aiden remembered Coach Hill's main instructions. "If the other team has the ball, go after it. If we have it, block for whoever needs it." That's about all Aiden knew about football.

The lead in the game went back and forth almost as much as the ball. The Beavers were ahead with less than a minute to go when Jason picked up a fumble and ran it for a touchdown. The game ended with the Bears 54 and the Badgers 49. That guaranteed at least a second-place trophy for the season.

The crowd surged onto the field to congratulate them. Aiden knew about half of the people there and was probably related to the other half. He had never felt anything like the adrenalin surge after their win, and he had never been treated like a hero before.

As they dressed, his best friend, Richard, came over. "Going to the dance?"

Aiden shook his head. "I don't know who I'd ask."

"I'm with you on that," Richard replied. "My cousin in Middleton set me up on a blind date, or I probably wouldn't be going."

After Aiden said he thought he might go hunting, some of the guys teased him about dancing with an elk. Aiden smiled. He knew it was all in fun, but he did wonder how he was ever going to find a girl he could date.

(To be continued)

24

A Silver Lining

Aiden reluctantly joined his high school's six-man football team because he was one of only six boys who could play, but finding a date to homecoming was impossible because he was likely related to every girl in the school. After winning the first game, Coach Hill warned them that the next team was better.

The day came that they were to play the Cougars, and they loaded into the van. Coach Hill turned to the team. "Men, we're playing a team that has many advantages. They have more players, they come from a school district with more money, and they are the undefeated champions for as long as I can remember. Sometimes they take cheap shots, but I don't want you responding in kind. Win or lose, we should be proud of playing an honest game."

Aiden turned to his best friend, Richard. "Have we ever beaten them?"

Richard shook his head. "Not that I know of. I've heard we have always gotten 45'd."

"What is 45'd?" Aiden asked.

"If the other team gets ahead by 45 points, the game is called," Richard said. "In fact, in all the years I've watched my brothers play, we not only got 45'd, but we also never scored a touchdown against them."

Their van pulled up to the football field, and they were soon warming up. The cheerleaders came in another van and started their cheers, always ending with "Go Bears!"

Aiden noted the stadium was bigger than at home but was filling up. It surprised Aiden how many traveled the distance from home to cheer for them, filling the smaller bleachers on their side. Soon, the other team came onto the field. There were eighteen of them, and every one of them had a sharp-looking new uniform. Aiden looked at his own baggy, stained uniform in contrast. In addition, almost every man on their team was bigger than Jason, the biggest player on the Bears team.

The game was not much of a contest, even though the Bears fought hard. Coach Hill was right about the other team taking cheap shots. By the second quarter, the Cougars had put in their second string, and by the third quarter, they had in their third. Toward the end of the fourth quarter, the Cougars had the ball and would 45 the Bears with one more touchdown.

That was when one Cougar player made an illegal hit on Richard. The player was ejected, but Richard also had to be helped off the field. Because of his gentle nature, Aiden wasn't the best football player, but what happened to Richard made him mad. Sam, the Bears only replacement, walked onto the field to fill the six-man quota. With his cerebral palsy, many from the other team laughed at his walk. That made Aiden even madder.

The ball was snapped, and the Cougar ball carrier burst through the Bear's line. Sam had been put far back in the backfield to avoid any contact, but the Cougar ball carrier ran straight for him. He obviously planned to run over Sam, even though he had an open field all around him. At the last minute, Sam dropped to the ground, and the ball carrier tripped over him and face-planted into the dirt.

Though Sam wasn't hurt badly, he had to be helped off the field. Richard had been bandaged up and insisted on coming back in.

As they lined up, Aiden was so mad about what happened to Richard and Sam that he could hardly contain himself. When the Cougars snapped the ball, Aiden smashed through their line, hit the ball carrier, and caused a fumble. Aiden picked it up and ran for a touchdown, with the Cougars so stunned they hardly even chased him.

The Cougars got one more touchdown before the buzzer, but the Bears weren't 45'd. Even though it was a loss, to Aiden's surprise, the Bear's fans acted like it was a victory. But Aiden had one other surprise coming. During the celebration, he suddenly felt a hand grab his. When he turned, one of the Cougar cheerleaders smiled at him. "You did a great job," she said.

As she walked away, he looked at the paper in his hand, and it had her name and phone number. Aiden smiled. Maybe she was related to all the boys in her school and couldn't find a date, either. Whatever the reason was, perhaps he would have a date for homecoming next year.

Standard Transmission

We just got a car with a standard transmission, an oddity in today's world. It hadn't been driven for quite a while, so I thought it would be good to have the oil changed. While they were doing the work, I settled into the waiting room and read a magazine. It wasn't long before they finished, and a young lady in mechanic overalls came to get me.

"I couldn't pull your car around for you," she said. "I don't know how to drive a standard."

I smiled. I recently read a story about a man who was sitting in his car in a parking lot reading a newspaper while he waited for his wife. Two men came up, jerked his door open, and threw him to the ground. They then jumped inside, planning to steal his car. But it was a standard transmission, and they obviously didn't know how to drive it, because they soon fled the scene, leaving the car as they found it.

How we got our new car is a story in itself. When I say "new," I mean new to us. The car has around 315,000 miles on it. But the story is worth telling.

There is a group on Facebook that shares stuff with each other. Instead of selling what they have, they offer it for nothing to someone who can use it. Likewise, when a person needs something, they are free to ask for it in the group. Whether they get it or not depends on whether someone has it to share.

My wife, Donna, is active in this group. She especially likes to share starts of plants, but as we have been moving into our later years and downsizing, there have been many things that Donna has given away.

At Christmas time, the group encouraged members to post something they could use, and everyone would attempt to fill the Christmas need lists as much as possible. A couple of young men independently posted that they could use a car. "It's freezing walking to college every day," one said. "If we can get a car," the other said, "we could share rides."

In response to their request, a lady posted that she had a car available. "It has 311,000 miles on it and is banged up a bit, but it runs well." She then went on to say that she couldn't drive anymore, and the apartment complex where she lived wanted the car removed from the parking lot.

At first, the boys were excited about it, but then she posted one other thing. "By the way, I forgot to mention that it has a standard transmission."

Immediately, all the chatter by the two boys about the car ended. Donna felt bad to think a lady had so kindly offered her car only to be ghosted on the posting, so she decided to write something to help the lady feel better. "It is so kind of you to offer a car," Donna said. "And standards are so fun to drive."

A few days later, the lady called Donna. "Would you like the car?" she asked. "I really have to get it out of the parking lot."

Donna picked me up, and we drove over to the apartment building. The lady gave Donna the keys, and I tried to start it, but it hardly flickered. It hadn't been driven for over a year, and the battery was dead. I had expected as much, so I brought a jumper. With a bit of power, it fired right up.

The car was a little dented, was missing a bumper, and it took me some work to get the trunk to latch, but it runs like it's new. It has become my car of choice when I drive around town and don't need my pickup to haul things. I have already put thousands of miles on it.

I guess the old adage is true. Knowledge is power. And it also helps in driving a car with a standard transmission.

Clutches and Lessons

Having received an old car for free because no one wanted it because it was a standard reminded me of something that happened when I was young. Back then, almost everyone drove cars with a standard transmission. Automatics were new and not too good yet.

My dad owned a farm implement business, and sometimes, when there was a lot of mechanic work to do, he would have me come help after school or on Saturdays. One Saturday, James, the head mechanic, put me to work on a tractor.

At lunchtime, everyone left, leaving me to watch over everything and promising to bring me something to eat. I was working underneath the tractor when I heard the bell indicating that someone had entered the shop. Footsteps approached before I could climb from under the tractor. As I stood, I looked up to see Rich Hamilton. He owned a car mechanic shop down the street and was a friend of my dad and James. He was a bit of a salty character, but I liked him.

"Where is everyone?" Mr. Hamilton asked.

"They all went to lunch and left me to watch over everything," I replied.

"What are you working on?" Mr. Hamilton asked.

"I just need to replace a clutch on this tractor," I said, pointing at it.

"Oh, don't get me started on clutches," he said. "They are the bane of my existence. People drive around with their foot resting on the clutch pedal, and then they can't figure out why their clutch wears out so fast. Well, duh. If your foot is even lightly on the pedal, it engages the clutch. And even a little will cause it to wear faster. Oh, everyone thinks they keep their foot off of it and say so when I ask them. But saying and doing are different things.

"You know Mr. Mathews, the farmer that owns much of the land southwest of town? He is one of the worst, always wearing out the clutches in that big pickup he drives. Then he blames me, saying I put in a defective one. So, one day, when he came in, I had had enough. I had put a new clutch in his truck less than a year earlier, and it was already worn out. I told him we should take a drive together so I could see what the problem was.

"On my way out the door, I grabbed a crescent wrench. 'What is that for?' he asked. I told him I wanted to use it on the problem if I saw it. 'That's all right, isn't it?' I asked. 'Well, of course,' he replied.

"Well, we got driving along, and sure enough, he was resting his foot on the clutch pedal. So, I reached over and whacked his leg with the wrench. 'What did you do that for?' he yelled. 'You told me I could use the wrench on the problem when I saw it,' I replied. Some people only learn from the school of hard knocks, or in this case, a hard wrench."

I smiled at Mr. Hamilton's story. We talked a bit more; then a big, beautiful pickup pulled up. It was Kevin, a boy my age. He wasn't a close friend, but we did have a P.E. class together.

Kevin walked up to Mr. Hamilton. "The secretary at your shop said I'd find you here. I want to talk to you about the defective clutch you put in my truck. It hasn't even lasted a year."

Mr. Hamilton looked at me and rolled his eyes. He then turned back to Kevin. "Why don't we go for a drive together so I can check out the problem?" He then turned back to me. "Can I borrow a wrench?"

I reached into the toolbox, pulled out a crescent wrench, and handed it to him. He nodded his thanks, and they left. I wasn't around when Mr. Hamilton brought the wrench back, but when Kevin came into P.E. on Monday, he was limping slightly. As he changed, I saw a big bruise on his leg.

"Where did you get the bruise?" I asked.

"Oh, that idiot Mr. Hamilton hit me with that stupid wrench you lent him," Kevin replied.

As Mr. Hamilton had said, some people only learn from the school of hard-knock wrenches.

Getting to the Hospital

Jack was a free, independent spirit. He loved to live life on his terms, which meant a fair amount of adventure. That adventure showed up in the only two vehicles he owned—a motorcycle and a plane.

Of course, most people wouldn't consider either of these "vehicles" in the usual sense of the word. Some might give in and concede a motorcycle as a vehicle, but almost no one besides Jack would think of a plane that way.

But Jack figured they were all he needed. He could go almost anywhere on his motorcycle. And if it was too far for his motorcycle, he would fly there.

But Jack's independent spirit ran up against a challenge the day he met Helen. She was, in many ways, a female version of himself. She was also independent, fiercely so. She didn't let people push her around, and she decided for herself no matter what others thought.

Jack asked her out. But to assess her adventurous nature, he told her it was a formal affair, then showed up on his motorcycle to transport her there. Helen didn't miss a beat. In her formal dress, she climbed on without even flinching. Then, for their formal date, he took her to the stockyard café by the cattle yards. Lots of cowmen were there, many smelling more like the cows they worked with than like anyone in a formal setting.

Jack and Helen were quite a sight there. The men were used to Jack doing what he chose no matter the norm, so they weren't too surprised at him in his unusual attire. But no one had seen a woman in a formal dress in the café. Helen didn't seem to care what others thought and was not bothered by the many staring eyes.

Jack was immediately smitten, and from then on, Jack and Helen were seen all over the area on Jack's motorcycle. But nothing could quite match the sight of the two of them in their wedding best, rolling along down the highway to the church—Helen's veil sailing out from under her helmet and flying behind her like a wedding train. And after the wedding, they headed off on the motorcycle for their honeymoon.

They had a lot of adventures together over the next year. Then Helen became pregnant. As the months went by and the room between Jack and Helen decreased on the motorcycle, it got less and less comfortable, especially for Helen. But her tenacity showed through as she continued to ride with Jack.

But then the day came that she went into labor. Jack helped her onto the motorcycle, and they sped off. But they had over fifty miles to go, most of it over rough back-country roads. They hadn't even gone a mile when the bouncing and the labor pains combined to a point that it was more than Helen could bear.

"Jack," she said, "you will just have to take me back and be the one who helps me deliver the baby."

Jack was adventurous, but even he had a point where he drew the line. Helping deliver a baby made him shudder. He took Helen back but reminded her that he had two vehicles. He helped her onto the plane, and away they went. It wasn't too long before they reached the only town in the area with a hospital, but the airport was miles away from any medical help.

In addition, Helen's pains were coming faster, and she told Jack it wouldn't be too long. Jack circled the airport once, then turned the plane downtown. He turned on all lights and everything else he could to get attention, then dropped toward Main Street.

Seeing a plane coming, cars veered off onto the side roads, and Jack made a perfect landing, then taxied up to the emergency room door. Helen was right. It wasn't even a half hour before their little girl was born.

And after the nurse placed her into Helen's arms, even before they announced the baby's name, Helen turned to Jack and said, "I think it's time for us to get a car."

Leaf Season

I love to garden. It helps me to feel at one with nature, and there is the added benefit of fresh food for my family. We have put our house up for sale, and I am building a new one. One challenge I have had is that over the thirty-five years we have lived in our current house, I have worked hard to make a nice garden.

It is soft, sandy soil, and I have hauled in loads of compost, leaves, and straw. It is rich in nutrients, and plants grow abundantly.

But our new place is packed clay. When it rains, every step you take is like walking in cement, and the soil accumulates on a person's shoes until they are carrying ten to twenty pounds of it on each foot.

After the soil dries, like cement, it hardens to the point that it is impenetrable. The first time I tried to dig a posthole in the hardened soil, I had to use a pick to break through the top layer. So, I am trying to put every ounce of mulch into my new garden area that I can.

The closest town to where I live is where I work. In the fall, the town allows people to put bags of leaves on the sidewalk, and the city crews pick them up. I decided I would pick up some of these for my garden.

This leaf season, as I like to call it, lasts about six weeks. My wife posted on Facebook that I'd like to pick up leaves. People started posting that they had some, and I hauled many loads. But soon, people just suggested that I take any that were put out along the street, and everyone seemed to agree that it was fine. I started loading my little pickup twice each day. After work, I would pile on a load and take them to our new place. Then, after working there all evening, I would go around and load another load and take it home to my current place.

I would unload that load into a pile to take down after leaf season ended. The next day, I would start all over. That way, I got two loads each day, six days a week. I could pile on about thirty to forty bags, so over the six weeks, the bags I have hauled number in the thousands.

Each time I loaded, I would pull through some neighborhoods until I found a good amount the city had not collected. But one day after work, a lady came out to talk to me as I piled on the bags from her yard.

"Do you work for the city?" she asked.

"No," I replied. "I just work for myself." I then explained what I did with the leaves. As I loaded, we talked. Another lady joined us, and she, too, asked if I worked for the city. Once more I explained what I was doing. As I was finishing loading and strapping down the load, a third lady joined us, and once more I had to explain what I was doing. But her eyes lit up like she understood something the others hadn't.

"Have you loaded from our street before?" she asked.

I nodded. "Quite a few times."

She then turned to the others. "Ladies, that answers the questions we had the other day at our block party."

"What questions?" the second lady asked.

"Well, you remember how Lana asked what day the city picked up leaves? We each said a different day."

The ladies smiled. The first lady said, "Mrs. Hansen insisted her leaves even disappeared on Saturdays when the city crews didn't work, and I mentioned that mine seemed to disappear overnight. No one could come to a consensus as to what day the city picked up from our street."

The ladies all laughed, and I asked if it bothered them. "Not at all," the first lady said. "It is nice to know they are going for a good use instead of being burned. The next time we see leaves disappearing at different times, we'll all know it is the Leaf Man."

I smiled. That was a title I had never had before.

Socket to It

Larry was excited the day his big gun safe arrived. He would put it in his basement and use it to protect many things. It had a high fireproof rating and could save many valuables, including irreplaceable family photos.

The day the truck arrived at his house, Larry was there to meet it. He had the driver back right to his door. When the driver opened the back of the truck, Larry was excited to see that the safe was even bigger than he thought.

The driver told him it was 1100 pounds. The driver lowered the safe with the drop-gate on the truck and used a pallet jack to work it through the door into the house. But after the driver left, Larry wondered how he would get the safe down the stairs. It was right at the top, but to move it would take some ingenuity.

Larry got the idea that if he could tip it off the pallet onto the stairs, it would slide down by itself. He got a crowbar under it but couldn't get one side more than an inch off the pallet. Then he had an idea.

Larry went outside and pulled his pickup near the door. He tied a board between the pickup's bumper and the top of the safe. He then slowly drove forward. He was excited to see the safe starting to tip. As it tumbled over and crashed down onto the stairs, the crunching of wood made Larry wonder if that might not have been the best decision.

The safe slid down the stairs okay, but the stairs were definitely going to need rebuilding. Larry was so excited to have the safe at the bottom that the needed stair repair couldn't even dampen his spirit.

The safe was mostly upright, and with a board behind it prying against a couple of cinder blocks, he was able to tip it up straight. It almost went all the way over, but it came back and settled itself into a standing position. But Larry couldn't think of a way to move it to its final position. He tried everything he could think of, and finally called his friend, Bob, for help.

Bob was an old engineer, but more than that, he was creative. He was more creative in his thinking than anyone else Larry knew. It didn't take Bob long to size up the situation, and seeing that they couldn't move it other than to lift one side a little, he sat down to think. As he did, he looked up and saw Larry's tool bench. Suddenly, his eyes lit up.

"Larry, do you have a bunch of sockets from a socket wrench set?" Bob asked.

Larry nodded. "Who doesn't?"

Larry retrieved them, and then, while Larry pried up one side, Bob slid some sockets under. They then did the same to the other side. When they pushed the safe, it almost took off without them. But the sockets on the push side quickly rolled out from under while the front ones rolled far enough under to drop the safe on that side to the floor. They lifted it again and stuck some more sockets under the front. They pushed slower this time, putting more sockets under the front and gathering up the ones that rolled out the back.

They continued this process and soon had the safe in place. They then pried it up and worked the remaining sockets out from under it. Some of Larry's sockets were no longer round, but he felt it was a small price to pay to have his safe nicely in place.

When Larry's wife came home and saw the safe in place and the damaged stairs, she turned to Larry. "And just what happens if we ever need to move?" she asked.

Larry thought a minute and said, "I guess we'll have to get another safe and a few more socket sets."

Love and Gratitude

Years ago, I was asked by the leaders of our congregation to be the music teacher to the children on Sundays. Many congregation members laughed when they heard about the assignment, but my children were the worst. My wife has a master's degree in music and performs a lot, but I seldom do anything musically in public. I might play the harmonica around the campfire and even played the harmonica for a choir number of Home on the Range once, but that challenged my comfort level. My children could hardly imagine me leading music.

As frightened as I was, I accepted the assignment. I loved the children. Previously, when the congregation leaders asked for volunteers to be substitute teachers at a moment's notice, I was the only one who volunteered. I loved the assignment and enjoyed my time with the children. But music scared me so badly that everything I tried was a failure.

Then, one day, the lady who oversaw the children's teaching on Sundays pulled me aside. "Daris," she said, "you are trying so hard. But one thing that might help is to remember that you only have one job when working with the children, and that is to love them. For years, you have shown you can do that. You continue to do that, and everything else will follow."

I thought a lot about that and realized I was trying to be something I wasn't. I had read every idea I found that people had for teaching children music, but those ideas didn't work for me because they weren't the way I worked with children.

I changed and started teaching how I teach best, and suddenly, things got better. I will share more on that in another story, but this week, having had Thanksgiving, I want to share a story of one little girl.

Mary was a darling little six-year-old. She was shy but loved to sing. But then her parents became embroiled in a nasty divorce. I watched as Mary started to withdraw and build a wall around herself. She wasn't the only child going through that in our community, but she seemed to be more devastated by what she was experiencing than any of the others.

I tried to give extra attention to any child I felt needed it, but I especially tried reaching out to Mary. Sometimes I would hear her softly joining in on her favorite songs, but mostly she just sat quietly. I always expressed my love for the children and tried to involve all of them, but especially Mary. Sometimes I felt she was slightly opening the barrier she had erected around herself, but I usually felt as shut out as everyone else in her life.

At Thanksgiving time, as part of our time together on Sunday, the children colored a picture of what they were grateful for to share with someone who meant a lot to them. The children all seemed to be preparing to share it with their parents. As we ended that day, I again let the children know I loved them, then sent them on their way with some popcorn and candy corn as a Thanksgiving treat. But as the other children left to show their parents their artistic endeavors, Mary held back.

She shyly brought her picture to me. I knelt so I could be at her height. I could tell she had put her heart into it, and I praised her for it. She smiled timidly, and I assumed she would take it to her parents. Instead, she put it into my hand and then threw her arms around my neck. She hugged me tight and cried a little as she did. I hugged her, too, and then she ran off to join her family.

I had thought the picture was of her and one of her parents. But, as I looked deeper, I realized it was her singing, with me leading the music. Then, in one corner, in small children's printing, I saw the words, "I love you, too."

And I felt very emotional as I realized that even though I felt I failed a lot in teaching music, the one thing that the children learned was that I loved them.

Overcoming Fear

I was asked to be the singing leader for the children in our small country congregation. It was an assignment that scared me to death. I hadn't had great experiences with public music performances, so I avoided it at all costs. But believing God would help me, I accepted.

It didn't start out well. After my first attempt, one little girl asked if I was going to be the music leader, and I said yes. "Well, that really stinks," she said. "You mess us up so bad."

But then the lady who oversaw the children's teaching at church and had requested that the congregation leaders ask me to take the music assignment told me that really my only job was to love the children. I thought, "I can do that," and it changed everything.

I thought a lot about the children. They were country kids through and through. The boys often wore cowboy boots and western-wear shirts to church. The girls often had calico dresses with their cowgirl boots.

So, the next week, when I started the music instruction, I said, "This week we are going to have some fun." I then told them we were going to sing one of their favorite children's songs in goat.

They looked surprised. "How do you sing in goat?" one little boy asked.

I then sang the first few lines, vibrating my voice like a bleating goat. The children laughed. Then we started over, and they joined me in a goat herd rendition like no one had ever heard before.

One little boy's hand shot up, and before I could call on him, he said, "Can we try it in cow?"

We did, and it went well. One girl asked for a chicken rendition. That one took us twice to make it sound reasonable. We attempted horse, but it sounded like a bunch of people all trying to clear their throats simultaneously, so we gave up on that one. But we had so much fun, and the children who had never heard the song before learned it in record time.

I realized that a lot about learning anything for children is fun. And we did have fun. When we sang songs that had the same word many times, every time we said that word, we did something. Sometimes we would stand if we were sitting and sit if we were standing. Sometimes we all shifted a seat to the right or left, and the person on the end had to run to the other end of the row.

We sang sacred songs much quieter and with more reverence, and I tried to teach the children that there are times for fun and times for respect. Using music that way was more effective in helping them understand than all the lectures I could give.

One week, as I thought about how I used the differences in the music to teach an understanding of sacred versus flamboyant songs, I realized that my little country children mostly only knew country music. With my wife having a master's degree in music, my listening library has increased dramatically since we were married. With that in mind, I decided to share different styles with the children.

I filled a paper with many different music styles like jazz, blues, rock, and, of course, country. I told the children that they got to choose the style, then I would choose the song.

One little boy raised his hand. "What does color have to do with music?"

"What do you mean?" I asked.

"You have blues on the list," he replied.

I laughed. "Yes. It goes like this."

I then did my best Louis Armstrong impression. The children laughed and joined me on the song. They soon understood many of the styles and would choose their favorites. Then, one day, a little girl chose opera. I sang the opening of a song, and then, as I started over, none of the children joined in. The older ones sat wide-eyed, while the little ones fell on the floor laughing.

"Hey," I said. "You're supposed to join in and sing with

me."

An eleven-year-old girl said, "If you sing like that, you sing alone."

So, we sang a song in country western. New is good, but so is the old tried and true.

Children and Musical Instruments

As I became more comfortable teaching music in my assignment with the children at our church, I decided that since they had learned styles of music, it might be fun to play some simple instruments. As I thought about it, I remembered learning to play a comb with cellophane wrapped around it when I was young. In fact, I became the king of the comb and played to accompany my grade school class to sing. I have even done a couple of YouTube videos.

For those who have not heard this most notable instrument, it sounds like a kazoo. Anyone can do it. You have to learn to hum and buzz your lips against the cellophane at the same time.

I went to the dollar store and bought a bunch of combs of different sizes. I took them and a box of cellophane to church. When I pulled them out, the combination intrigued the children. I didn't give cellophane to the youngest children for safety reasons, but they still got a nice comb. But the children who were around four years and older had a chance to play one.

It only took about fifteen minutes for every child to learn, some even faster. A few needed special help, but soon all got the hang of it. We then played a few of our favorite songs. As church ended, every child took a comb home with them, and the older children received some extra strips of cellophane. The older children were all buzzing out their favorite songs on their way to the parking lot. It sounded like hives of bees had made the church their home.

I promised the children that if they would bring their combs back each week, we would play some songs together. The following week, most of them had their combs with them. One little boy didn't. "My mom took mine and hid it," he said. I had extras, so he was quickly back in the orchestra.

One father told me his two children played their combs

incessantly all week. "If I end up killing you, I'll be acquitted by reason of insanity," he said.

I promised the children they could play at least one comb song for the community Christmas party, but I wanted something even more oriented to the season. I had searched the internet for inexpensive bells, but everything was way out of my price range. Then I came across a website that talked about conduit being cut in lengths to make different notes.

I bought some conduit and cut a bunch of each desired length. I drilled holes in them and put different colored strings for each note through the holes to hold them. I then bought some large nails and ground the pointed ends off. When I finished, I examined them.

"I think I better ream them out, or someone will get a finger stuck in one," I told my wife, Donna.

"I don't think that will happen," she replied.

That Sunday, I hadn't passed them out to the children for more than a minute before one little boy had his finger stuck in his. I took him to the bathroom and got soap on his finger to get it out. For obvious reasons, I also had to make a rule that if anyone used their chime to whack someone else, they lost it for the day.

Donna made a chart for each Christmas song we played with colored dots related to the string colors so the children would know when to hit theirs. I grouped them by age and notes. It sounded amazing for a children's chime orchestra.

The desire to ding the conduit was so great that I found I needed to let them smack them with the nails for about thirty seconds before we could settle in and play the songs. I'm sure when they were all hitting their chimes at the same time, the dissonance made people wonder what we were up to. But with a little practice, we also played them for the Christmas party, and the parents were all complimentary.

It's amazing what can be learned and what fun can be had with a few simple items.

New Assignment

There is an old saying that the only constant in life is change. After a rocky start teaching music to the children at our church, it became one of the greatest experiences I have ever had. But eventually, the day came when our congregation leader, whom we called Bishop, or the bishop, asked me to visit with him in his office.

"Daris," he said, "how long have you been teaching music to the children?"

"Around four and a half years," I replied.

The shock from my response showed in his face. "Wow!" he said. "I remember when we asked you to take the assignment, and we said we expected to keep you in it for only a year. But you've been so good that I didn't realize how long it has been. You have really loved the children, haven't you?"

I nodded. "I feel like children are God's gift to the world, and we show our gratitude to Him in how we love and train them."

"And they have loved you, too," he replied. "That is why asking you to take on a different assignment is hard, because I know how much they will miss you."

"I will miss them, too," I replied.

He leaned toward me and put his arms on his desk. "We might have kept you there if it wasn't for another assignment we desperately need you in. We have a large group of boys who are now scouting age. You know them well, because you taught them music. Your work in scouting is legendary, and these boys need your skill in the outdoors and mentoring for their lives. Will you do that?"

I nodded. "If that's where I can be of the most value, I will give my whole heart to it."

He smiled. "I know you will."

The bishop wanted someone ready to replace me, so it was a couple of weeks before they announced the change. When I went for the last time to teach the children, there was a solemness as I started.

"Well," I said, "when you children get old enough to move on into scouting and other teenage things, I have had you choose your favorite songs to sing for your last day with us. So, I guess today it's my turn."

As we sang a lively, fun song, few joined in, and some started to cry. I finally had to stop, not able to sing myself. One small girl ran up, threw her arms around my leg, and cried. I picked her up into my arms.

"Why are you going to leave us?" she asked. "Don't you love us?"

I nodded. "Of course I love you, Annie. But sometimes in life, we are asked to take different assignments. There are some boys who need me with them now."

"But we need you, too," she said.

"I'll still be around," I replied. "And your new music leader will love you. And maybe I can sub if she needs someone."

Everyone cheered up a bit after that, and the singing was more enjoyable. As we were ending, one of the children's organization leaders came up to where I was.

"We have a special present for you," she told me. "We knew you were leaving, because we were asked to suggest a replacement. We didn't tell the children other than to say we wanted to get a gift for you. Everyone, including the children, has chipped in for it."

She presented me with a beautiful, framed picture of Jesus, with children gathered around him, and a smaller one with a hanging ring on it. "We thought you might like to hang the smaller one on your Christmas tree," she said.

Many of the children rushed up to give me a hug, and I struggled to hold in my emotions. When I went home, I hung the ornament on our tree. It reminded me that Christmas was about God's gift to the world of a very special child. The ornament seemed very appropriate.

Then, after getting my emotions under control, I readied myself for my new scouting assignment—something familiar, but something always adventurous and challenging.

(Note: I have a book about my adventures in scouting called, "The Last Man Off the Mountain".)
https://publishinginspiration.com/Products/?ID=6)

The Ultimate Compliment

My assignment in our church congregation had changed from teaching children music to scouting, and I had been a scout leader for about six months. My wife, Donna, was the new leader of the children's organization. One Sunday, she asked me to assist her.

"I want you to come help me with something I am trying to teach the children," she said.

When I asked her what my assignment would be, she was vague about it, telling me she would let me know when the time came. I was always happy to help with the children, so I readily agreed, even though I didn't know what I would be doing.

When I walked into the primary, the children got excited. They thought I was there to teach music. I had substituted for their current music teacher whenever she needed, but Donna quickly told the children that I was there for a different purpose. That made the children curious, but no more curious than I was.

When it came time for Donna to do her learning activity, she asked for a volunteer and chose Katie, one of the oldest girls. She then had someone take Katie out into the hall and blindfold her.

While Katie was in the hall, of the other forty-five people left in the room, Donna chose a few children and an adult, to play the part of good people. She then told the other forty-two that they were to play the part of evil people. She marked a place in the room and said that was heaven, and those chosen to play good people were to help lead Katie there. Those chosen to play evil people were to lead her anywhere else. But no one could touch her.

Katie was brought in, and soon, the overwhelming noise from those chosen for the evil part had her bumping into walls and tripping over things. I felt bad for her but still didn't know my assignment. Finally, when Katie was about as far away from the

49

designated heaven spot as possible, my wife said I could stand in that spot and direct Katie there, but only in a whisper.

I thought, "This is impossible. There is no way she will hear me through all the noise from the opposite end of the room."

But I had an advantage I had forgotten about. When the children would have a lesson like this where they were all excited, and then time was turned to me to teach music, sometimes it was impossible to get them to calm down for singing practice. A suggestion people gave me was to do a "wiggle song," which was an active one like "Head, Shoulders, Knees, and Toes." They said it would take out the wiggles. But that never worked for me. They just grew wigglier.

But one day, as the leaders did their learning activity, I thought of a story that would blend with it. As I tried to get the children calmed down to sing, I said, "Let me tell you a story." Most of the children hurried to their seats. I continued to use this technique, but I found if I whispered, every child rushed to their seats and sat quietly so they could hear the story.

So, I no sooner had whispered, "Katie, listen to me," then Katie spun around to face me. All the other children also rushed to their seats, ready for a story. It took a second for Donna to get them back to their exuberance in trying to influence Katie's direction, but it was to no avail. In all that noise, once Katie locked onto my voice, she followed my directions, no matter how softly I spoke or how loudly everyone else did.

After Katie was safely at the heaven spot and the blindfold was removed, Donna asked her, "Why did you pick Daris's voice out from all the others, especially when he was so quiet?" Before Katie could answer, another girl did. "Because we trust him, duh."

Donna then taught the children that God tries to reach out to us, but his voice is like a whisper compared to the noise and influence of the world around us. "We need to learn to hear his promptings and trust Him," she said.

As I left that day, I felt I had also learned something else. It is a wonderful thing to know that children trust you.

Shared Traditions

I pulled up in front of our house, coming home in the dark from work, and my heart was flooded with feelings. As I looked through our bay window, it was as if I could see our family gathered around on Christmas morning, opening the stockings, the children squealing with delight at the new treasures they found.

My wife and I always got up the minute we heard the children stirring on Christmas morning. While she put on the finishing touches to make everything just right, I made a full breakfast. I cooked scrambled eggs, bacon, sausage, and hash browns to go with the favorite cereals the children had requested. While everything cooked, I mixed up various kinds of juice. When everything finished cooking, I called everyone to breakfast and then cooked piles of toast.

With ten children plus foster children, it was like a small army that descended the stairs, rushing to the table. The rule was that everyone had to eat a hearty breakfast, and then they were free to eat all the candy they wanted until dinner in the middle of the afternoon. This was the only day we allowed free rein on the candy, and we found the substantial breakfast kept them from overindulging and getting sick.

No one was allowed to even peek into the living room until everyone was ready, so once breakfast was over, the children gathered to wait at the door. When I opened the door, they flooded into the living room and found their stockings neatly laid out on the furniture from oldest to youngest. Each boy had a buck deer on his, and the girls' stockings sported a beautiful doe.

As the children dug into their stockings, they found things like new socks, pajamas, hair items for the girls, and a comb or pocketknife for the boys. Then they would find toys, candy, and a new calendar with nature scenes for their room.

Once the stockings were emptied, with only my wife and mine left, we moved to the presents. Each year, the next child in order was the Santa and chose the presents from under the tree and took them to whomever they were for. We did presents one at a time, slowing things down considerably and making the fun last longer. Everyone could enjoy seeing what others received.

Before Christmas, I took each child for "date time" where they got to choose a place to eat out and buy a present for the person whose name they had drawn that year. I enjoyed the time with them, and it was fun on Christmas for everyone to see who had drawn their name and what that person had gotten them. Of course, I often had suggestions for the little ones. Otherwise, the boys might get a doll from a little sister or the girls a truck from a younger brother.

Once all the presents were opened, we sat down to watch whatever new movie I had purchased for the family that year. Then we usually went outside and built a snowman or went sledding before coming in for a wonderful ham dinner.

But as I sat in my pickup, looking through the window with all those memories coming back, it all seemed so distant. Our children are all grown and gone, most with their own families. They are scattered from Alabama to California and Alaska. Christmas is not the same without children and their excitement. I didn't even go to the effort of pulling our Christmas tree from storage, so my wife finally bought an eighteen-inch one at the dollar store.

Then, just before Christmas, our daughter called. "Dad and Mom, come down for Christmas."

We joined them on Christmas Eve and helped act out the Christmas story as we always used to. We got to see the excitement of their children, who couldn't sleep. And on Christmas morning, we saw the children trying to down a big breakfast quickly so they could get to their stockings. Then they followed the stocking and one-at-a-time present opening as we used to do.

It is hard getting old and having certain wonderful parts of life fade away, but it is fun to see many of the best traditions shared and continued to the next generation.

Toys, New and Old

The week before Christmas, our five-year-old granddaughter was extremely excited when her mother let her call me. Our grandson was calmer about it, as he always is. And the little two-year-old was only excited because she knew her sister was. But there was one other person in the family that was excited for a different reason.

"I'll be glad when the children have new toys," my daughter said. "Maybe that way they will leave the utensil drawer alone. I'm so tired of rewashing them every time we get ready to eat."

I don't know what it is with utensils, but they seem to fascinate children. Our children were no different. We would come into the kitchen to find forks, spoons, and butter knives spread everywhere. Often in their place in the drawer, we would discover Tinker Toys, Lincoln Logs, or something else the children were playing with previously.

I'm not sure it's utensils in particular that fascinate them. Children seem drawn to whatever they aren't supposed to have. If we told our children that the paper drawer was off limits, that's exactly what they wanted to play in. If it were a sock drawer we wanted to keep neat, they would imagine the ban on it was because it was fun and immediately imagine all the socks as puppets or pets to play with.

The fact of the matter is, adults are the same way. The banister outside my office was painted recently. Soon, there were signs that said, "Wet Paint, Do Not Touch," everywhere. I must admit I felt tempted to touch it, but I didn't. But students walking back from class to my office with me would inevitably feel it, and when they pulled their finger back to look at it, it was covered with wet paint. They would always say, "Oh, my goodness, it is wet," as if someone had just put the signs up because they had nothing better to do.

We are not the only creatures that are drawn to things that are off-limits. Almost all are. An example was a story I wrote about some hay we couldn't get our cows to eat. If we stuck it in their manger, they wouldn't touch it. But we found if we put it in a fenced corral, leaving the gate so they could knock it down, they would get in and slick up every morsel of hay.

So, Christmas came, and our grandchildren were thrilled with their fantastic new toys. My daughter was pleased not to have to wash the utensils over and over.

"They just play happily in their room now," she said.

On New Year's Eve, I called my daughter. We had gotten a new phone for my son-in-law, and I wanted to make sure they were able to get it working.

"Oh, yes," she said. "We should have told you. The minute the phone store was back open after Christmas, he got the information he needed to get it working."

Suddenly, there was a clattering noise in the background. She said, "Dad, hang on a minute. I need to check on the children." A few seconds later, I heard her from the other room say, "Seriously, it hasn't even been a week yet!"

When she came back on the phone, she said, "Dad, you're not going to believe what the children are playing with." Actually, I would, but she went on to tell me they had scattered utensils all over the kitchen. "And I was just getting ready to make dinner," she said.

I laughed as I thought about a certain little two-year-old girl. Our Christmas tree had no decorations on the lowest three feet. We had tried to explain to her that the ornaments needed to stay on the tree, which made her want to play with them more. We tried to put a fence around the tree, but she always found a way over or around it. Finally, we had to just leave the bottom empty of things a small child could get her hands on.

It's good to know my grandchildren are normal and that they take after their mother.

Inspections

Building a home of your own can be a challenge. One of the hardest parts is passing all of the inspections. There is plumbing, framing, insulation, electrical, and the list seems to go on and on. I have spent many hours poring over the different code books to make sure everything was right. But there always seems to be something I miss.

A friend who has retired from construction said his boss always had them leave something undone so the inspector would find it and not search for some nitty gritty item. I tried that, but the inspector found something small and missed the item I left undone.

I appreciated the inspectors, not because I enjoy knowing I have something more to fix, but because it helps me feel I am building everything right. But there was one thing that I had to redo that was strenuous to change, and I wondered if it was needed.

My new place is a shop with an apartment above. The stairs between the floors are U-shaped, with two landings between the three segments. Two of the three segments measured right on, but the bottom segment was a quarter inch low, both where it started from the ground level and where it connected on the first landing.

"You're going to have to raise the whole stair segment a quarter inch," the inspector said.

I didn't complain. It was his job to find the errors, and my job to fix them, but internally, I felt sick. I would have to cut the nails that connected the stairs to the walls on both sides of it, along with the ones tying it to the landing. He also wanted the board under the stairs at the bottom to be treated since it would rest on the cement. I didn't know anywhere I could get a treated board that was a quarter-inch thick.

After the inspector left, I got to work. I started cutting the nails with my reciprocating saw. Two friends had helped me build it, and it was solid. I went through three saw blades before it was loose from all sides. However, even when I was sure it was free, it wouldn't move. Not only was it heavy for me to lift, but it was also binding against the two side walls. Taking the walls apart was not an option, since they bore other structures.

After three days of working on it, it finally moved. Now I needed a board to slide under the lower end. I took the thinnest treated board I could find to a friend who planed it down for me. Then, while I lifted the stairs, my wife stuck the board under the lower part. I had put marks at the top to which I needed to raise it so I wouldn't go over. I didn't want to have to lower it again.

Once everything was in place, I put in a few screws to keep it from moving. I didn't want to put in nails until it passed inspection. It did pass the next inspection, so I tightened everything down.

Sunday, as I talked to my two construction friends at church, I told them of the ordeal. They didn't have the same opinion I had that inspectors were there to help me make the building better. "I think they actually train them on ways to annoy people," one said.

I laughed. They both had been to Peru and visited Machu Picchu, so I asked, "Did either of you climb Machu Picchu Mountain?" They both said they did.

Machu Picchu Mountain is a tall mountain that overlooks the historic site. The path to the top is comprised of stairs carved into the rock. There is no standard for them. One stair will be six inches, and the next eighteen. I think some were even as much as two feet in height. Their height depended on the way the rock was on the side of the mountain.

"I'm sure those building the stairs on the mountain didn't have inspectors telling them the stairs weren't even," I said.

One of my construction friends laughed. "Oh, I'm sure they had them. But when the inspectors said the stairs wouldn't pass inspection, the builders probably just took them to the top of the mountain and sacrificed them."

I laughed, but I'm still grateful to have someone who ensures that I build it correctly.

The Renaissance Fair

Now that their children were raised, Lydia wanted to do something she had always hoped to do: form a quartet. It would not be just any quartet. She wanted to have her three friends join her at Renaissance Fairs and sing Celtic songs. But there was just one problem: they needed someone to accompany them. That was where her husband, Don, came in.

Don was more reserved than his wife, but he was also an accomplished guitar player. Lydia approached him about her idea.

"But won't it be a little strange with me traveling with four women to these types of gatherings?" Don asked.

Lydia laughed. "What would be strange about it?"

Don thought about it, and realizing how much it meant to his wife, he agreed. The women started coming over a couple of days each week to practice. Don realized his guitar playing didn't match the style the women were trying to sing, so he listened to lots of Celtic music and practiced until he felt he had more of the sound they were looking for.

Summer came, and they drove to their first performance. The women were excited and talked nonstop as they traveled together in the minivan. After they arrived, they unpacked and prepared for their first show. It turned out well, but Don knew it wasn't perfect. However, for a first performance, they could be proud of the job they did. The people cheered and clapped, especially after the last number when the women did some crazy Celtic dancing.

As they were packing up, a young man came up to visit with Don.

"So, the program says you are all from Utah," the man said. "Are all four of these women your wives?"

Don was embarrassed, wondering how many others might think that. "No," he replied. "One is my wife. The others are her friends. In fact, Mormons don't have more than one wife anymore."

Don ended up having a pleasant visit with the man, who was extremely curious why a group of "old people" would choose to do such lively music and dancing.

"It has always been my wife's dream to do this," Don said. "She's enjoying some things she never got to do when she was younger."

They went to quite a few fairs that summer. The women had so much fun that they decided to kick it up a notch. The next year, they made dresses with skirts that stuck out four to five feet all around them. They were excited to try them out.

But they hadn't even left home yet when the problems began. Trying to fit four skirts that were about ten feet in diameter into a minivan without crushing them was no small feat. Eventually, the dresses were loaded, and the group packed into the remaining space.

Once they got to the fair, another issue arose. The tent they brought to change in would only hold one lady at a time with a dress that large. They barely had their costumes on in time for their performance. That was when a third problem appeared. The small stage would not accommodate their four dresses and Don, too. Don took a position beside the stage, but the ladies still had to be careful not to knock each other off the platform, and dancing was impossible.

But then the challenge arose that was the final straw. When they finished their performance, they all desperately needed to use the bathroom. But the small outhouses positioned around the fair were not big enough for even one lady in her dress. They eventually found a handicap one, and with tucking and shoving, each made their way inside one at a time. By the time they finished, there were a few people in wheelchairs lined up for their turn.

As they headed for home that day, Lydia spoke frankly. "The fairs are fun, but the dresses have to go."

Everyone heartily agreed.

Showing Gratitude

Sherrie had just moved into a new neighborhood the last week of October that year. She and her husband were young and recently married, and she couldn't wait to get to know the people around her. She thought she would go for a walk each day and try to meet everyone.

But having grown up in the South, she wasn't ready for what happened the following week; the snow started falling. Sherrie thought it was beautiful and could hardly wait to try her hand at a snowball, sledding, or the many other things she had heard so much about. She donned her coat and headed outside.

There wasn't much snow yet, but she was able to make a snowball. That was when she realized how cold it was. It didn't take long for the frigid breeze to drive her inside. She was still determined to get out and walk, but in her first attempt, she quickly realized that she didn't want to get too far from home. A short walk was all she could endure before seeking warmth.

The cold drove the neighbors in as well, but not permanently. Most of them were older, and they didn't seem too inclined to want to play in it. But they weren't afraid to get out and work for hours in temperatures Sherrie couldn't stand for more than about fifteen minutes.

She decided she still should get some exercise, even if she couldn't meet her neighbors. She decided she would go to the local Y.M.C.A. and walk the small indoor track there. But it was freezing, and she thought she might wait until the snow and cold eased up. But it never did. The snow kept coming, and the temperatures kept dropping.

She couldn't believe anyone would live in a place like this. Her husband had grown up there, and he didn't seem bothered. He told her most people there were used to it. She felt trapped, like a caged animal, and she desperately needed to get out, even if to just go shopping. But the day she determined that cold and snow wouldn't hold her back, the wind picked up, and suddenly, there were drifts across her driveway taller than her car. She felt like crying.

Then something else happened. Suddenly, one of her neighbors was clearing her driveway with a snowblower. She hadn't seen such a machine before, and she watched out the window with great fascination. She and her husband only had shovels, and the snow hadn't been that deep. But this machine was making quick work of the huge drifts.

When he finished, she felt a sense of relief that surprised her. She no longer felt trapped. Whether she stayed in or went somewhere, at least she could choose. And she did choose to go to the grocery store about ten blocks away. After almost sliding through a stop sign, she decided that short distance was plenty.

When she got home, she felt much better, and her heart was filled with gratitude to the neighbor who had cleared her walk. She made some homemade bread, took a bottle of jam she bought at the store, and bundled up as best she could. With the bread hot from the oven, she headed over to the neighbor's house.

An older gentleman answered the door. She handed him the bread, and he thanked her. As he invited her in, he asked if she minded if he ate it hot right then. Sherrie assured him she didn't mind and smiled as he led her back to the kitchen to meet his wife. They invited her to join them, and they all enjoyed a pleasant visit as they ate some bread and jam. But then, at one point, the woman asked Sherrie why she brought over the bread.

"It was my way of saying thank you to your husband for clearing the snow from my yard," Sherrie replied.

The man shook his head. "It wasn't me."

Sherrie must have looked shocked because the man laughed. "All of us old guys bundled up for winter look the same."

But Sherrie learned something else that day. She didn't have to go somewhere to get out. A hot loaf of bread would get her out of the house and into a neighbor's warm home where she could meet others. Besides, with all the different snow blowers that cleared her driveway that winter, she never knew which neighbor it was each time it happened. So, she just thought she'd say thank you to everyone.

Just One of Those Days?

✦

We are trying to move things to our new place so we can sell our old one. I have a million things to do, so I thought I'd start by taking our tent trailer and parking it on our new property.

I checked the tires, and one was a little low. I hoped to hurry so I could spend the entire day at our new place and finish the last of the electrical wiring in our shop. I got out a small air compressor and quickly filled the tire. Donna, my wife, and I headed on our way, but we only went a few miles when the tire I filled decided to blow. I drove slowly to the side of the road, riding on the rim.

Donna had some things she absolutely had to do at our new place to prepare for a meeting she had later, so I unhitched the trailer and took her down. I drove the forty miles back to get the trailer but realized I didn't have a jack. I drove the forty miles back down, got the jack, and then drove back to the trailer.

The jack was rusty, so I had to work on it for a while to get it to loosen up. Finally, I got it working and jacked the trailer up. I got the tire off and put on the spare. The spare held for about a mile before it, too, blew.

Once more, I jacked up the trailer. I took the two tires with me. I went to the tire store near our new home, and the repairman looked at the tires.

"There is no way we can repair these," he said. "You will have to replace the tires."

He checked their inventory, and they didn't have any that size in stock. He informed me it would take a little while to get it from the other store. Just then, Donna called. She needed to go to her appointment and preferred the nicer vehicle since it was a business meeting.

"No problem," I said. "I'll just switch to the pickup."

We had parked the pickup earlier at our new place. So, I left the tires, took my vehicle, and switched it to Donna. I thought I'd take some time to work on some electrical wiring. I barely got everything in place to hang a light when the tire store called and said the tires were ready.

I drove the truck to pick up the tires, then drove the forty minutes to the trailer. I went to put the tires on but realized the jack was in the car Donna was driving. I called, and she was done with her meeting, so I drove down to our new place and got the jack. I drove the forty miles back to the trailer.

I got it jacked up and put one tire on the trailer. I then put the spare on the spare rack. I was frustrated and wondered what else could go wrong. I was about halfway to our new place, going around seventy on the highway, when the last tire that was not new exploded. It almost threw me off the road.

I got as far off the road as I could and started trying to change the tire. But the lug nuts were too tight, and I couldn't budge them. I searched throughout the truck for something, but there was nothing. I drove to our new place and got a pipe. After driving back, I put the pipe on the tire wrench and barely had enough torque to turn the nuts. Finally, I had the tire changed and was on my way.

By the time I pulled in at our new place, the sun was already down. As I parked the trailer, I thought about all the wiring I had planned to do that day. I went inside, and Donna was packing up.

"I'm all done," she said. "Let's go home."

It was just one of those days.

Date Night Social

At the religious university where I work, COVID took a heavy toll on everyone. I'm not talking about sickness or death. I'm talking about a social toll. Students, sequestered away for a year, struggled to reconnect outside of social media. They also seemed to have lost confidence in their ability to make friends in an in-person situation.

For that reason, the religious and university leaders were determined to help correct this challenge. They set a night as "Date Night" for all the students on campus to get a date, and the bill would be on the university. It would be just over a week before Valentine's Day, and there would be ice cream and lots of activities, including pickleball matches led by the university president and his wife.

It was big talk on campus for the three or four weeks leading up to that night. Students in my classes brought it up every day. Roommates were encouraged to help set up others in the apartment on blind dates if they struggled to find someone on their own. I even had students come to talk to me before and after class.

One young man asked me how a guy would go about asking a girl out.

"Have you ever tried?" I asked.

He shook his head. "With COVID we couldn't really meet in person, so there wasn't any opportunity. Then, when it was over, it was a habit to just stay home."

"The first thing you do is simply to visit with a young lady and get to know her," I told him.

"But what do I say?" he asked.

"Don't you ever visit with girls on the phone or on Facebook?" I asked.

He nodded. "But that's different."

"Not really," I replied. "Just talk about the same things you do there. I see you visit with your math group in my class. When there's a lull in the conversation, just ask a girl if she has a date to Date Night. If she says she doesn't, ask her if she'd like to go with you."

It wasn't long before he had a date with a girl in his group. I saw the interaction, but he came to tell me about it anyway. I high-fived him, and he went away smiling.

The Tuesday before the big night, we had a campus-wide devotional, and the university president reminded everyone to get a date and come have fun. Later, at a faculty meeting, he told us that a young lady came to visit with him after the devotional and could hardly contain her excitement.

"I've got to tell you what happened," she said. "When you made the announcement, I was sitting by the love of my life." She paused and smiled shyly. "Actually, he doesn't yet know he is the love of my life, but he is. Anyway, I was sitting by him, and I asked him if he had a date for Date Night, and he said he didn't. Then he asked me if I had one, and I told him no. He then asked, 'How about you go with me?' President, I can't believe it. He asked me out!"

The president shared in her happiness; then she turned to leave. Instantly, she turned back and said, "When we get married, I'll send you an announcement." Then she rushed off to catch up to the love of her life.

The college president said, "We all need to have that kind of confidence and enthusiasm."

In a meeting with the vice presidents, the president asked how many they should plan on for the ice cream. The consensus was that 2500 would probably come. The president said, "Let's assume 3000 and plan for 3500." They were way wrong. There ended up being more than 7000 students there. They ran out of ice cream in about fifteen minutes. Staff members were dispatched to buy ice cream at all the stores, but they still couldn't get enough.

Listening to my students talk about it in class the next day, I knew it was a big hit. The young people had connected in ways some of them never had. One girl summed up how many of them felt.

"It feels like COVID is finally over," she said.

The Test Question

It was finals week. Most students were busy taking tests and trying to do their last clean checks before they left. Others were preparing for graduation and moving on to the next part of their lives. As a professor, I was giving tests, grading them, and spending lots of time visiting with students who had been less than diligent but still hoped to pass.

I was busy grading linear algebra tests when my phone rang. I answered it and immediately recognized my niece's voice.

"Uncle Daris," she said, "could you help me and my roommates with something?"

"What?" I asked.

"Well, when we moved in this semester, we all hated the showerhead in our bathroom. So, we bought one that we all liked better. But the apartment managers will expect the original one put back on for checkout."

"If the one you bought is better, don't you think they would be okay with it?" I asked.

"I said we liked it better," she replied. "The original one was meant to save water, but it hardly put out anything. It was like showering under a dripping faucet. The one we bought put out a lot more water. I'm sure they would want their water-saving one, but we don't have any wrenches to switch it."

"I'd be happy to help," I said. "I'll bring my wrenches to work tomorrow. I have to give a test at ten but should be free early in the afternoon."

"That would work perfectly," my niece said. "We will be here packing."

I arrived at their apartment just after noon the next day. My niece invited me in, introduced me to her roommates who were there, then led me past piles of boxes in the living room. When we got to the bathroom, she handed me the shower head they wanted to have reinstalled.

"How did you install it the first time without any wrenches?" I asked.

"My roommate, Valentina, had her boyfriend do it. But he's not her boyfriend anymore, so she doesn't want to ask him."

"I'm happy to do it," I replied.

While they continued to pack, I changed the shower head. When I returned to the living room, they were hauling boxes to their cars. They had loaded some boxes extra heavy, and they couldn't lift them, so I hauled the heavy ones for them.

As I came in after one trip, another roommate had returned from taking a test. She was crying. My niece was trying to comfort her. When my niece saw me, she introduced me to Valentina.

"Valentina just took a test, and she is sure she bombed it," my niece said. She then turned to Valentina and said, "My uncle is a professor. Maybe he'll know."

Valentina nodded and turned to me, speaking with a strong South American accent. "I thought I was doing well on the test, and then I got to the last question. It was so confusing that it made me wonder if I didn't know the answers as well as I thought. I'm afraid I did horribly on the test."

"Can you tell me the question?" I asked.

"It was something about chucking wood or something," she replied, "and I don't remember ever talking about chucking wood."

"Was it, 'How much wood can a woodchuck chuck if a woodchuck could chuck wood?'" I asked.

She looked shocked. "You know the question?"

"What were the answers?" I asked.

"One said, 'One Log.' Another said, '2 cord.' And the last one just said, 'choose me, choose me,' which I know was a dumb answer."

I laughed. "The phrase is just a common, crazy thing we sometimes say in the United States. I'm sure the professor was using it to give you some free points. He probably expected you to choose the last one, but I'm sure he'll give you points for any of them."

Valentina smiled and dried her tears. Then she asked, "So how much wood can a woodchuck chuck if a woodchuck could chuck wood?"

I smiled. "I'm sure we'll never really know."

I Don't Speak Spanish

My mother learned to speak Spanish in her youth and fell in love with the language and the people. She became so fluent in it that the courts would call her to help them when their regular translator was gone. But we never spoke Spanish in our home, and those of my siblings who learned it did so after they went to college.

My mother was ninety-six and was a resident of an assisted living center. I visited her often, but one day, she was particularly upset.

"Why didn't you tell me you could speak Spanish?" she asked me.

"I can't," I replied.

"Oh, come on," she said. "I watched a program on TV where you were speaking, and you were talking in Spanish. And your Spanish was superb."

"I'm sure they must have dubbed it," I replied.

"Why should they have dubbed it when you were speaking it so well on your own?" she asked.

"It wasn't me speaking it," I replied.

"Now, now, son, I know your voice," she said. "I know very well it was you. Oh, you sounded like you had a bit of a cold, but you often do this time of year."

"But, Mom, it wasn't me speaking."

"Sure it was. They announced your name and everything. And, of course, I could see you."

"Seriously, Mom, I don't speak Spanish," I said.

"Well, you should. As good as your Spanish is, you really should speak it more."

I decided to try another approach. "Mom, tell me what I was speaking about?"

She told me all about it in great detail. When she finished, she said, "It was a wonderful talk."

"Thanks, Mom. But I gave that talk a year and a half ago. Do you remember when we came and got you and took you up to the big auditorium at the university? Then, afterward, we all went to the student center to eat. That was when I gave that talk."

Mom thought a moment and then said, "I do remember that."

I smiled, thinking I was finally making some headway.

"So why didn't you invite me when you gave the talk in Spanish?" she asked.

"Because I never gave the talk in Spanish," I replied.

"So, where did you learn to speak Spanish?" she asked. "I learned when I was in Texas. Did you learn when you were away in New York?"

I sighed. "I never learned Spanish."

"So, have you learned any other languages besides Spanish since you left home?"

I decided to try an attempt at humor. "Well, when I went to college to become a computer scientist, I learned the Fortran programming language. Since then, I've learned Pascal, C, C++, Java, Java Script, and a dozen or so others."

- "Wow!" she said. "I didn't know you were so fluent. I haven't even heard of most of those. I know Java is what they speak on an Indonesian island, and Fortran is what they speak in France, right?"

I realized that my attempt at humor had fallen worse than flat, and I didn't know what to say. Just then, one of the aides came in.

My mom turned to her. "Do you want to hear something crazy? I'm ninety-six, my son is sixty, and I only now learned that he speaks fluent Spanish."

"Oh, how nice," the aide said. "I know how much you love speaking Spanish to everyone you can."

The aide was there to help Mom go to bed, so I decided I should leave.

Mom smiled as she said goodbye. "And next time you come back, let's speak some Spanish together."

So, on my way home, I decided I better go to the bookstore and get a Spanish-English dictionary.

My Red Badge of Courage

I try to give blood as often as I can. According to the Red Cross, my blood is not only one of the most needed, but it also has a rare characteristic. I can't explain it, but it has something or lacks something that makes it critical for children. I've tried to understand, but I don't remember what it is any more than what my blood pressure means. I'm a mathematician, but those numbers go by me.

I especially try to give blood when the Red Cross comes to the university where I work. It's hard for me to get away to go somewhere else, but I can just schedule my appointment during my lunch break and slip over there. I usually have pleasant conversations with those working there.

"Did you understand everything in the questionnaire?" the lady asked while checking me in at the drive.

"I haven't heard of half of the diseases it asked about," I replied.

"That's good," she said. "That means you haven't had them."

As she poked my finger to test my iron level, she said, "Soon, we will have a machine where we can measure this without even poking your finger."

"What I want is for them to create a machine that will take my blood without me having to have a needle in my arm," I said.

The lady laughed. "That might be a while."

"I think they have one on Star Trek," I replied.

She nodded. "Some of those science fiction gadgets would be great, wouldn't they?"

"I think there might be a downside," I said. "If they made it so easy you didn't feel anything, what would stop somebody from setting a machine up on the street and taking people's blood as they walked by without them knowing it?"

The lady smiled. "That's an interesting thought."

They got the needle in my arm, and it wasn't too long before I was done. I pressed the cotton against the wound on my arm, and then the lady looked at it. "It isn't bleeding at all. Do you still want the red wrap around it?"

"Of course," I replied. "How else can I make people feel sorry for me?"

She laughed. "Is that the reason you come to give blood?"

"Well, that and the cookies," I replied. "But it's a darn hard way to get a cookie."

One thing about giving blood at a college is there is usually the enticement of pizza. After a little food, snacks, and juice, it was time for me to head to class.

As I was preparing everything for class, a girl asked, "What's the bandage on your arm?"

"It's my red badge of courage," I replied.

"You're what?" she asked.

"My red badge of courage," I answered. I could tell she was unfamiliar with that book, so I continued. "I gave blood today, and I hate needles, so I call it my red badge of courage."

"What would ever make you want to give blood?" a boy asked. "They don't pay you any money, do they?"

"No," I replied. "But I get something better." I explained about my blood being used for children. "I understand that most people who can give blood for children lose that ability somewhere in their mid-twenties. But I've been able to do it since I was a teenager. I like to think of it helping some child."

"Well, they'd have to have something really good to get me to do it," the boy said.

"They had a lot of wonderful pizza," I said.

The boy looked at his friend in the seat next to him. "How about we head over right after class and see if they have an opening?" The friend nodded.

I laughed. "And don't forget to get your red badge of courage while you're at it."

A Glaring Problem

✦

We were waiting to go on stage, and some performers were talking.

"So, how old are you?" Susan asked Tina.

"Thirty-eight," Tina replied.

Turning to the third person in their group, Susan asked, "And how old are you, Dawn?"

"Thirty-seven," Dawn replied.

"How old are you?" Dawn asked Susan.

"Forty-nine," Susan replied.

"Wow!" Dawn said. "You don't look anywhere near that old."

Tina nodded. "I thought you were even younger than either of us."

"How do you keep yourself looking so young?" Dawn asked.

Susan appeared a bit embarrassed, but she reluctantly answered. "Botox."

"I have always had my doubts about it," Dawn said. "But it appears to work."

"Do you like it?" Tina asked.

"Yes and no," Susan replied. "I do like how it makes me look younger, but I don't like the other results."

"Then why did you do it?" Tina asked.

"Some friends I went to high school with talked me into getting it done with them," Susan said. "But no one told me about the side effects, not even the doctor."

"Is it painful?" Dawn asked.

"No, nothing like that," Susan replied. "It's just the unexpected consequence I hadn't realized would happen."

"Like what?" Tina asked.

"Well, since I became a mother, when my children did something wrong, I would glare at them. I didn't even have to say anything, but my glare told them they needed to knock it off. I even got so that I would glare at my husband when he was in trouble. But after I got Botox, I found the upper part of my face frozen without wrinkles or anything."

"But isn't that what you want?" Dawn asked.

"I didn't want them to always be there," Susan replied. "But I didn't think Botox would eliminate my ability to wrinkle my brow or scrunch up my eyes when I wanted to.

"The first time my husband left his clothes lying around after I got Botox, I tried to glare at him, and he laughed. He said, 'It looks like your face can't decide whether it's mad or happy. The top part of your face says you're happy, but the bottom says you're ticked off.'

"His laughing made me even madder, but when I looked in the mirror and tried to glare, I realized he was right. Even though I was mad, my face seemed comically unconvinced.

"My children were no different from my husband. I could glare at them, and they just continued doing what they were doing. I have three teenagers, and they definitely need a mother who can glare at them now and then to help them change their ways. Now I have to tell them I'm mad at something they are doing, and it doesn't have the same effect. In fact, one day they were all laughing, and when I peeked around the corner, I caught them each trying to imitate my face while saying they were mad. Then, the others would laugh. I never knew how humiliating it would be not to be able to have my face show my true emotions."

The other two ladies smiled. "I have never thought about what it would be like to be unable to show my emotions," Dawn said.

"The doctor told me that the treatment would only last a few months," Susan said. And when it does, he will be the first one I glare at, and it will feel good."

Time's Up

⊹

For church on Sundays, my wife, Donna, and I work with college-age youth. The church meetings are held on a church-owned campus, so on Sundays, classrooms become Sunday School rooms, and faculty offices become ecclesiastical offices.

I thoroughly enjoy my work with the youth on Sundays. As a teacher at the same university, my weekdays are filled with grading, helping students who have not done their homework, and encouraging and prodding in any way I can to help them pass my classes. But on Sundays, I can just enjoy being in church with them. On other days of the week, we also participate in activities with them.

The youth are so vibrant and excited about life. They see so much of the adventure that awaits them in their future. But sometimes they just need someone who has been there that they can talk to. Often, they don't need your advice, just someone to listen to them as they figure out the answer on their own.

On some Sunday mornings, both youth and adult leaders meet to determine the needs of the young people we work with. This meeting always starts with a five-minute devotional that is rotated among the group. As would be my luck, my day fell on Daylight Savings weekend in the fall.

That is not the best weekend for anything in church. Even though people gain an hour, everyone's sleep schedule is thrown off, and people still come to church tired.

I thought for a long time about what I could share that would be inspiring, especially on that weekend. The thought needed to be kept as close to five minutes as possible so we could get to the business at hand.

I feel that, at least for me, something is more meaningful if it is shared as a story taken from one's own experience. The problem is, if I share a story, I tend to get off topic, and then the time passes quickly.

I was determined to stay within the allotted time, so I first chose a topic where I could get the point across quickly. I put a clock in front of me and practiced multiple times, ensuring I stayed within the time limit. The first few times, I got to the end of the time and was only halfway through the thought. I kept cutting and cutting until I came in at five minutes, almost to the second.

On that weekend, I got up early and did one last practice. As Donna and I headed off to the meeting, I felt confident it would be just right. We all sat in a circle, so I chose a seat so I was positioned facing directly toward the only clock in the room. I looked at it, and it had not yet been set for daylight savings time. It was still an hour off, but that didn't matter, because I just had to look at the minute hand no matter what hour it was on.

The meeting started, and the time was turned to me. I stood up and looked at the clock to get my bearing on when the five minutes would end. However, before I could say a word, something happened that I hadn't expected.

The clocks on the campus are all controlled from one central place. Those in charge can set all of them at once, but the only way they can set them back an hour is to spin the minute hand around the clock eleven times. As I looked at the clock, the minute hand started spinning around, circling the clock about every twenty seconds.

I stood there stunned, so everyone else turned to look at the clock. I finally found my voice and shared the thought as I had practiced it. I was sure it was close to the five minutes allowed. But when I finished, one leader smiled and said, "That was the fastest twenty-three-hour-and-five-minute devotional I have ever heard."

And so it was.

The Spray Bottle

✦

My wife, Donna, is a band instrument repair person. She has been repairing instruments for twenty-one years. She has become proficient at it. As a member of NAPBIRT (National Association of Professional Band Instrument Repair Technicians), she has shared, and has had shared with her, some interesting stories and images, such as a trumpet that a person ran over and flattened totally, then brought it in, thinking it could be repaired. As one technician said, "It went from a C trumpet to an A flat trumpet." One day, a young band instrument technician shared his story.

Lance had gone through some of the best training a person could have for band instrument repair. There are two ways to get this training: a trade school or an apprenticeship. Lance had done both. He then went on to work for a music store for a few years before setting up his own shop.

Previous to starting his own business, the shops he worked in had all been set up for him. He just had to do the work. It was exciting for him to set up his own shop. He could put the tools and materials where he wanted them. And one thing he wanted was to have the things he used within easy reach. Something that really annoyed him was that the school and the shop he worked in had some things so far away.

He had grown up with a father that wanted his wood shop a particular way, and every wrench had its spot, which was labeled. Similarly, the shops he worked in had a certain spot for everything, and he was required to put it back in its place when he was done.

Of course, Lance made sure he had the safety equipment in place that he had been trained to have. Nearby was the water spray bottle, the most crucial tool for any little flame that might get out of hand. As a last resort, a fire extinguisher hung on the wall.

Lance liked his convenient little shop. He didn't have to go far for the things he consistently used. One of these was the rust remover. In the other shops, it was on a shelf a distance away from his workbench. Though it was only five steps away, it was an annoyance to go get it and then have to put it back. It seemed like every instrument that came in was stuck in some way and needed something to break through the corrosion.

Lance did an excellent job, and business quickly picked up. The efficiency of his shop made it so he was able to do a few extra instruments each day and make more money.

One day, Lance was brazing a piece of metal with a butane burner. To keep the instrument piece from getting scratched or dented, he had it sitting on a rug piece on his workbench. But in the process, he got the fire a little too close to the carpet. This was not the first time this had happened. Most technicians he knew used something like a carpet under the instruments when they worked on them, and that was how he had been trained.

Lance didn't even get excited. He just reached for the ever-constant water bottle to put it out. But just as he hit the spray nozzle, he realized that instead of water, he had grabbed a can of WD-40. Suddenly, a fireball engulfed the area in front of him, including the instrument he had been working on.

He quickly grabbed the water spray bottle and put out the fire in short order. Maybe putting the flammable chemicals a distance away and walking to get them was a good idea. Perhaps others had done something similar, and that was why they had them where they did.

Lance moved the chemicals across the room, then went to change his underwear, grateful that was the only incidental damage of the mishap.

April Fools Test

We were coming to the end of our third unit in College Algebra, so I reminded my students that we had a test coming up. "It will open next Friday, April 1st, so make sure you work on the test review."

Rich, a boy in my class, started to laugh. "Oh, that's good. A test on April Fool's Day."

I shrugged. "That just happens to be when the unit ends. I don't control the calendar."

He laughed even more. "Oh, that is so funny."

The other students stared at Rich but said nothing. His social skills weren't the best, so it wasn't new. More than once, we had been right in the middle of an important discussion when he had turned to the person next to him to talk about something totally off-topic.

One day, I was showing the students the easiest way to think about logarithms when he said to the boy beside him, "Did you catch the basketball game last night? I can't believe an eleventh-seed team could knock off the first-seed one. I guess that blows my bracket."

The other boy looked frustrated because he was trying hard to take notes and understand the material. I paused, as I usually do when students are loud in class. In the silence, students almost always realize they are disturbing the class. But Rich was an exception. He seemed oblivious to the fact that everyone was staring at him and continued talking about the game, and he didn't have a low volume.

Finally, I called his name. I had to call it again before he heard me.

"Rich, we would like to continue with the lesson," I said.

"Oh, don't mind me," he said. "I was just telling Kevin

about the game last night."

"Yes, I know," I said. "We all do. But I think Kevin is trying hard to understand the math."

Kevin nodded.

"Oh, I can help with that," Rich said. He then loudly started to explain it to Kevin.

Rich was bright, and what he said was mostly right. However, that was his one challenge. He missed details, and usually, they were important. Often, the small details can make or break parts of math questions.

It took me a while to realize Rich's problem was that he was too into his phone. I have a no-phone-or-computer-in-class rule unless we are using them for the day, but I realized he was sneaking it out behind his textbook. That was what was causing him to miss the information.

The week after I announced the test, I allotted time at the beginning of each class for questions from the test review. More than half of the review questions were asked over the few days leading up to the exam. I worked all that were asked on the board.

I noticed that Rich had his phone open behind his book during those times and was paying no attention to what I was doing. I had reminded him about the rule a few times, and even though he lost points, he continued. I finally gave up bringing it to his attention.

Eventually, the test day came. I stood in front of the class with a stack of tests. "Okay, everyone, put away your books and everything except for a pencil, blank paper, and calculator."

Rich started laughing. "Ha, ha, ha," he said. "April Fools."

But his countenance changed as I passed out the test, and everyone started working on it. "You mean the test is real?" he asked.

"I told you it was," I replied. "And we worked problems from the review all week."

"But I didn't prepare," he said. "I was sure it was just a joke."

Kevin turned to him. "It is, but only on you."

Putting it all Together

The phone rang, and Jacob picked it up. The person on the other end explained what they had called about, and once he understood, he apologized: "I'm sure that's not what Mary meant." They talked briefly, and then, after he hung up, he went to find his wife.

Though they were both in their late thirties, they had only been married just over a year. Both of them had wanted to marry years earlier, but neither of them had found the right person. When Jacob met Mary, he immediately knew she was the right one for him. She was kind, loving, and had a wonderful, gentle nature about her.

But she had one weakness, and that was probably what had turned off most guys. He was sure that was also the reason for the phone call.

Jacob entered the kitchen to find Mary crying and making a delicious-smelling dinner. "Mary, what are you doing, and why are you crying?" he asked.

Mary turned to him with tears pouring down her cheeks. "You remember my friend Jenny Smith? I'm fixing dinner for her family. She died today."

"Why do you think that?" Jacob asked.

"It had to be today," Mary said. "I saw her just this morning."

"So, why do you think she died?" Jacob asked.

"Because I saw it in the paper," Mary answered.

She handed him the paper, and he turned to the obituaries. "But, Mary, this isn't her."

"It says Jenny Smith."

"But there are probably thousands of Jenny Smiths," Jacob replied.

"But it's her picture," Mary said.

"I don't think so," Jacob replied. "This lady may look a lot like her, but it is a picture from the woman's early years because the obituary says she was born in 1928. That would make her around ninety-six, and your friend is only in her thirties."

Mary turned to him, her tears subsiding. "So, Jenny is okay?"

Jacob smiled. "She must be. She just called me, and I don't think heaven has phone service."

Mary smiled through her tears. "I'm so glad she's okay."

"Mary, did you stop to think about the fact that you saw Jenny this morning and the paper would be printing obituaries from yesterday and before?" Jacob asked. "There is no way you could have visited with her in the morning and read her obituary later the same day."

"I didn't think about that," Mary said.

That was Mary's one weakness. She didn't always put things together and make logical decisions. He had talked to her about it, but she couldn't understand the problem.

"What did Jenny say when she called?" Mary asked.

"She said her family was concerned about the message you sent them," Jacob replied.

"I was only expressing my condolences at her passing," Mary said.

"I know that," Jacob said. "But since Jenny is still alive, some of her relatives took your note saying you hoped she would rest in peace as a threat."

"Why?" Jenny asked.

"Have you ever seen a movie where a mob boss is mad at someone and says to his hit man, 'May he rest in peace?' That is his way of saying they are to knock the person off."

Mary shrugged. "I didn't mean it that way."

"Jenny knows that, but her family didn't," Jacob replied.

Jacob wanted to talk more about Mary trying to think things through better, but he knew it would have to wait. Mary had the dinner ready, and they needed to take it to Jenny and her family while it was still hot.

(To be continued)

Putting it all Together

(Conclusion)

Jacob was concerned about his wife, Mary, because she didn't always think things through logically before making decisions. This had caused a problem when she sent a note to the family of her friend saying she hoped her friend would rest in peace, because her friend hadn't passed away. If Mary had thought about it more, she would have realized that.

Jacob feared Mary's impulsiveness might get her into real trouble someday. He decided to talk to her about it to try to convince her to attempt to analyze things more before reacting.

Mary didn't seem to understand his concern. "What kind of things could cause a problem?" she asked.

"Do you remember when we were getting married, and my mother told you that she had always wanted a daughter and was grateful to now have one?" Jacob replied.

Mary nodded.

"Do you remember how you took that to mean my mother was pregnant?" Jacob asked.

"Well, that was what it sounded like to me," Mary said.

"But, Mary, my mother was only referring to you and having a daughter in the form of a daughter-in-law."

"How was I supposed to know that?" Mary asked.

"My mother was nearly sixty when we got married," Jacob said. "It would be almost impossible for her to be having children. It took almost two months to quell all the commotion you caused trying to throw that surprise baby shower."

"I was just excited for her," Mary replied.

No matter what Jacob said, Mary couldn't see it as a problem. He tried to think of some way to help her think about it more. Then, one day, he saw Mary's cell phone sitting on the table in the kitchen, and he had an idea.

He took a picture of the phone so it was easy to tell that it was on their own kitchen table. He then filed it away where he could use it at the right time. It wasn't long before that time came.

Mary was going shopping, and after she finished, she planned to go to a meeting she had each month with some friends. She was the secretary of a lady's organization and took minutes on her cell phone. She would then come home and transcribe the minutes from her phone into an email she sent to everyone to recap what they had discussed. She took her assignment seriously and never missed a meeting.

After she left the house, Jacob waited until he felt Mary had just enough time to reach the grocery store. He then texted her the picture of her cell phone sitting on the kitchen table. Everything worked just as he expected.

It wasn't long before Mary returned home and dashed into the house. She ran into the kitchen and looked at the table. Not finding her phone there, she frantically searched all the places she normally put it. Soon she came to Jacob, who was reading the paper.

"Honey, can you tell me where my cell phone is?"

Jacob calmly looked up from the paper. "Why do you ask?"

"Because you just sent me a picture of it sitting on the table, but it isn't there!"

"And how did you get the picture I sent?" Jacob asked.

"It came in on my cell phone," Mary replied.

"Then where was your cell phone at the time you were looking at the picture?" Jacob asked.

"On the table," Mary said.

"How could it be on the table if you were holding it in your hand looking at the picture?" Jacob asked.

Mary pondered that, and it slowly sank in. She looked at the phone in her hand and smiled sheepishly. Then she left for her meeting.

Mary did try to think things through a bit more after that.

Putting on a Positive Spin

A cousin of mine just passed away. Becky was a great lady, and I'll miss her a lot. She was also a writer, having written for farm magazines for years. She also wrote children's books and books about people's encounters with Bigfoot. But one of the things I will miss the most is the way she could find something positive in the hardest of situations.

Becky was about three years younger than me, while her oldest brother, Kelly, was born only a year after me. When we were very young, Becky would tag along with Kelly and me, and I just viewed her as Kelly's annoying little sister. But as time went on, my opinion changed.

It wasn't that she didn't still tag along with us, but her spunk and willingness to try almost anything grew on me. She could do nearly anything we could, and sometimes even better. As we grew into our teenage years, we became even better friends.

But as life often does, our paths diverged when we went our separate ways to college and other things that took us away from home and family. We both married and moved far away from each other. We seldom connected, and it was usually through other family members that I learned what was happening in her life.

I didn't know the challenges she faced in life. She had eight children, but her marriage wasn't the best. To say her husband wasn't kind to her or the children is an understatement. I didn't know that until I heard about her divorce. We lived far apart, so we still never saw each other.

Then things changed. She moved to southern Idaho, and though we were still hundreds of miles away from each other, we took the time to catch up on what our families were doing. Then, one day, she called and asked if I could help her family move to a town only about forty miles from where we lived. I was glad to help, and on the appointed day, my wife, Donna, and I rented a trailer and headed down to help Becky move.

My pickup is an old flatbed. I have built wood sides on it, and frankly, it looks like something right out of Beverly Hillbillies. It took all day to load the truck and trailer. Once we got almost everything on and stacked high above the cab, we found an old recliner that family members couldn't bear to leave behind. I got on top, and they hoisted it up, and I strapped it right on top of the load. We could have been the very model of that old sitcom if we only had a granny to sit in the chair.

Becky squeezed into the truck cab with Donna and me, and her children, with the oldest driving, packed into the car. All the way to their new place, we shared stories from our lives. Never once did I hear a complaint. Instead of talking about her divorce, she referred to it as her new start in life. Instead of referring to the job she just lost as downsizing, she talked about a chance for new employment opportunities.

Her death this week was unexpected, but all her children made it to the funeral. In visiting with one of her daughters about how her mother was always positive, I loved what she told me. She said the divorce was hard, and her dad got almost everything monetary. However, Becky got what she wanted most: the children. But with little money, they found themselves homeless.

"We were definitely homeless," her daughter said. "But mom called it camping."

I smiled. That was Becky, always finding the positive in everything. I'm sure she is making her little corner of heaven just a little brighter.

Bagpipes

I had only been a faculty member at the university where I work for a few years, when I was sitting in my office and heard a strange sound. I couldn't quite tell where it was coming from, but it sounded like it was coming from my ceiling.

I decided to ask some of my colleagues if they heard it, too. I headed to the first open office down the hall, but as I did, I realized the sound was getting louder the closer I got to the outer office door. So, instead of bothering my colleague, I decided to leave our office complex and step into the hall.

The minute I opened the door to the hall, I recognized the sound. Someone was playing bagpipes. I do like bagpipes, though I must admit I only enjoy listening to them in short intervals—about a half hour is my limit. I stood in the hall and listened for a while, then I went back to work.

From then on, at least one day each week, I would hear the bagpipes and go to the hall to listen. I never heard other loud sounds in the building, so I reasoned it must be that bagpipes have a resonance that carries into the open space above the false ceiling.

After listening for a few weeks, I decided to meet whoever was playing them. So, the next time I heard them, I followed the sound until I got to an office on the opposite side of the building from mine. I was further amazed at how far the sound carried.

I hated to interrupt, but I just had to meet him, so I knocked. When he answered, I recognized a new professor at our college.

"Am I bothering you?" he asked.

I shook my head. "No. I just wanted to come to meet the talented bagpipe player."

He laughed. "I'm sure some people wouldn't put the word 'talented' in the same sentence as bagpipes."

I told him about going into the hall from our office complex to hear him better. He told me he practiced in his office at the college because practicing at home was too much for his family and neighbors. We had a pleasant visit, and then I returned to my office so he could continue.

One day, when I went into the hall to listen, the college dean approached the math department. He looked at me quizzically, seemingly wondering why I was standing there.

"I'm listening to the bagpipes," I told him.

He laughed. "Is that what it is? I was about to head over to the Biology Department and remind them that they are supposed to euthanize the cats before dissecting them."

I laughed. Some people don't really appreciate bagpipes.

One day I ran into the bagpipe player's wife at a community concert practice. I told her that the orchestra needed a number that included bagpipes.

She laughed. "My husband actually tried to do something like that once. He got the idea that his bagpipes would sound good with piano accompaniment, along with the mellow sound of a tuba. But it didn't work."

"Why not?" I asked.

"Bagpipes can't be tuned. When he played, the tuba player could kind of tune to him, but the piano couldn't. And if the tuba player tried to tune to the bagpipes, he was very disconnected from the piano. It was just too much chaos."

"But I thought bagpipes were all about dissonance and a controlled cacophony of sound," I said.

"That is probably a good way to put it," she replied. "But adding other instruments takes it a little too far."

I smiled. It is true that I have never heard any other instrument play with bagpipes besides other bagpipes. But I still like them, at least for short intervals.

Not Part of the Group

I was in my junior year in college when I learned it wasn't always good to be part of the popular group. I was taking a senior-level class in numerical analysis, a mix of computer science and mathematics. We had to learn the best algorithms for solving all sorts of math-related problems, mostly in calculus and differential equations, and then write Fortran programs to solve those problems.

The class had around thirty students. I was the only junior and the only married student in the class. However, I soon found myself outside of the group in another significant way.

A few of the students suggested we have a meeting. I thought they planned to have a study session but quickly realized there was a much different reason for the gathering. The students who organized the meeting asked if any of us were having trouble with the amount of work and the programming. Everyone was.

"Well, no one has ever gotten better than a B in this class," one boy said, "but we have a plan. What if all of us refuse to do the work? The teacher can't fail all of us. That would make him look like a failure of a teacher. And no one wants to work this hard their senior year."

They discussed it as a form of protest and urged us all to make a pact to join in. My social standing in the class was already dismal. Everyone knew I was married, and I was seldom included during visiting time before or after class. And when they planned a fun activity, I was always informed I wasn't invited because it was only for singles.

However, even though I knew it would destroy any chance of being part of the group, I knew I couldn't do what they asked for two reasons. First, I didn't feel it was right, and second, I worked hard to earn money for my tuition and to take care of my family, and I was determined to learn all I could, even if it was hard.

I told them I wouldn't do what they asked, and as I turned to leave, their mockery of me was vicious and relentless. I went to the computer lab to work on the next assignment, feeling very much alone. But then another young man from the class walked in. He was shy and seldom said anything, so I didn't know him well.

He took the chair at the computer terminal next to me, then turned to me. "I refused to do what they asked, too. I was afraid to say anything, but when you walked out, it gave me the courage to leave as well."

I introduced myself. He then told me his name was Richard. We talked for a while and decided to work as study partners, something the teacher encouraged.

The next day, the teacher was surprised when Richard and I were the only ones who came to class. He started a bit late, thinking others would come. We never told him what the group had decided, but it didn't take him long to figure it out.

Some of the others would come now and then, but their attitude was not one of learning but one of defiance. With only two of us interested in learning, we had more individual time with the teacher and completed everything that was required, something few had ever done.

Richard and I finished our last projects early during finals week and turned them in. With only two to grade, the teacher posted the grades before the last day of class, which was set aside for any final questions. Richard and I got A's, and the others failed. All the other students showed up for class that day.

When the teacher asked for any final questions, one boy raised his hand. "I see that you failed over ninety percent of the class. Does that make you feel good?"

Even though the boy's tone was abrasive, the teacher seemed unruffled. "A grade is nothing more than me stating how well I feel you know the material. If you can show me you know the material, I'll change it. If you can't, I won't."

"What if no one knows the material?" the boy asked, glaring at Richard and me.

"Then all would fail, and I would be forced to make that declaration," the teacher said.

"But you're making it so we won't graduate," one girl said, almost in tears.

"No," the teacher replied. "I'm not making it so you won't graduate. You are."

As with many things in life, what I learned that semester was far more than the class material.

The Test Review

We were about halfway through the semester, and it was time for the second test in my C programming class that I taught. I told the students that I would do a test review during the next class period to give them an idea of what I expected.

When the next class period came, my class was empty. Forty-eight students were enrolled in it, so I knew it was more than just one or two being sick or forgetting. I walked next door to the computer lab. I could see most of my students were there. I announced that I was starting class, but none of them moved toward the classroom. Instead, they just grinned and continued with what they were doing.

It didn't require any stretch of the imagination to know what was going on. I remembered, that while working on my degree, all of the students in one of my classes, except for two of us, decided that if they skipped class, the teacher couldn't fail all of them. It appeared my students felt I couldn't give them the test if I didn't do a review. I realized there was just one thing to do.

I faced the empty classroom and said, "The first question is going to be about using pointers to return items from functions." I then wrote a sample type of function and return values on the board and explained it in full detail. I then moved to question two. My explanations were more thorough than usual, and when I asked for questions, there were none. Of course, no one was there to ask.

I went through the test concepts one problem at a time, as I always did, and was getting near the end of the hour. I was just finishing the information on the last question when a grinning student stuck his head in the door. He grinned wider, seeing the empty room, but his grin disappeared when he saw what I was doing.

He quickly disappeared, and I was erasing the board when

the students came rushing into the room.

After they took their seats, I said, "Next time will be the test. Anyone who misses without a good reason will get an automatic zero. Any questions?"

One boy raised his hand, and when I called on him, he asked, "How can you give us a test when we haven't had a review?"

"But I just did a review," I replied. "I told you it would be today."

"You gave a test review to an empty classroom?" another boy asked incredulously.

"My job is to teach," I said. "That is what I am paid to do. No matter how many students do or don't come, to earn my wage fairly, I am expected to carry out my assignment. Me fulfilling my assignment is not dictated by whether or not you fulfill yours."

A girl shook her head in disbelief. "Professor Howard, you're strange."

"Thank you," I replied. "Class is excused. I'll see you all on Friday."

When Friday came, no one was absent. The test results were much lower than usual, and the students were relatively subdued when I passed them back at the beginning of the next class. One of the girls in the class looked like she was about to cry.

"Okay," I said. "I believe in both justice and mercy. You have seen the justice part. Now it's time for the mercy."

"You're going to increase our grades?" one boy asked.

I shook my head. "No, you are. Mercy is not always free. You can earn it." I then handed them each a piece of paper. "On this paper," I said, "you will find a list of programs you can write along with possible points you can earn if you choose to do them. The points cannot total more than the points you lost on the test, but you can decide which programs you do and how many points you gain."

Many of the students groaned at the extra work, but most did it. The programs were meant to challenge them and make them dig a little deeper. By the end of the semester, the enhanced skills showed in their work.

But more important than the programming skill they gained, they learned a lesson about life.

A Mother's Day Visit

A friend of mine made a Mother's Day Facebook post that touched my heart.

Steven was not a perfect child—far from it. He got into lots of trouble and did things that were very wrong. His actions led him to friends like him, and together they continued down a path leading them to worse things.

Steven's parents tried to help and direct him in any way they could. They tried to promote wholesome activities and better friends. But nothing they did worked to pull Steven from the path he was on.

Eventually, Steven was busted for drug use and sentenced to prison. Prison life was hard, and he had some challenging times. Through it all, his parents did what they could to encourage him and let him know they loved him.

Steven would sometimes get the desire to change, but the path was slippery, and the pressure in prison would make him drop his resolve and revert to his old ways. But then, one day, something did occur that changed his life; he got word that his mother had passed away.

Losing one of the few people who loved him unconditionally hit him harder than even his prison sentence had. His mother had always been there for him, and Steven knew she loved him no matter what he did. Being in prison, he couldn't even attend her funeral to express his love for her.

As he thought of her love for him, that love did something nothing else could do. It steeled his resolve to change, and nothing could sway him from that determination. He started working to make the changes he needed in his life to move down the right path. It wasn't easy, but any time he faltered, he would think of his mother, and it renewed his determination.

Steven eventually worked up to the point where he could be part of a work crew. He gained experience that would benefit him when the time came for him to start a new life outside of prison. The day eventually came that he was released on parole, and his father welcomed him home.

Steven faced new challenges of fitting back into society. As he looked for a job, though no one said it directly, he knew the many rejections were because of his prison record. But one day, the boss of a construction crew, who desperately needed help, decided to give him a chance.

Steven worked hard and showed he was dependable. He quickly learned different skills and soon became the crew member everyone turned to when they had questions. He also worked efficiently and often accomplished more than two or three other men.

Each day brought new challenges, but Steven never looked back. The memory of his mother's love for him kept him moving forward until his life settled into somewhat of a normalcy with regular day-to-day challenges.

This Mother's Day, Steven posted a picture of his mother's tombstone with a caption that said, "Mom and I had a nice visit today."

He then told about sharing with her the ways his life had changed. He said he was sad that she had never seen anything but the troubled side of his life, having not lived long enough to see him become a positive, contributing member of society.

As Steven talked to her, he said he cried a lot. Those tears washed away much of the pain and regret he felt for the sorrow he had caused her. He said he only wished she could see him now.

As I read his post, I thought she probably can, and she's smiling.

Grandchildren and a Strange Grandpa

One of the highlights of my week is on Sunday when one of our daughters, Trissa, does FaceTime with us so we can talk to her and our grandchildren and see them simultaneously. With our children and grandchildren spread from California to Alabama to Alaska, we don't get to see them near as much as we would like.

My problem is that any call does strange things to my brain. When I'm not on a call, I can think of a million things I want to visit with my children and grandchildren about. But the minute we connect, those things are all gone, and I can't think of anything to say.

That can be good when others want to talk, because I can just listen. But if they ask how I'm doing, I usually can't think of anything new. However, sometimes I have the opposite problem, saying things like how I write and getting strange looks from my grandchildren.

One day, when Trissa called, she wanted to show me how much her two-year-old daughter was learning and talking. She prompted her. "Tell Grandpa about the things you like."

My darling granddaughter just stared at me on the phone. I think she inherited my phone-call-equals-empty-thoughts dilemma.

My daughter tried again. "Claire, do you like macaroni and cheese?"

Claire nodded. "Yes."

"Do you like pizza?"

Claire again nodded and said yes.

"What else do you like?" Trissa asked.

"Bampa," she replied.

"That's sweet," I said.

Trissa nodded. "Yes, but I want her to show you all the new

words she's learned." She tried again. "Claire, do you like going to the park?"

"Yes," Claire replied.

"Who do you like to play with at the park?" Trissa asked.

"Bampa," Claire said.

"How about your brother and sister?" Trissa asked. Claire nodded. "And who else?" Trissa asked.

"Bampa," Claire replied.

It hardly mattered what Trissa asked about. Claire's answer was almost always the same. It seems on the phone she is just like me.

Trissa gave up and let her five-year-old, Emily, take the phone. I asked her how she was doing. She told me about her progress in learning to read, including new books she could mostly read on her own. She told me about her friends and things she liked.

When she finished, she asked, "How are you doing, Grandpa?"

I had worked so hard all week moving and mounting cupboards and loading a piano that my whole body ached. Without thinking about the fact that I was speaking to a five-year-old, my brain kicked into allegory mode.

"Well, I have worked so hard and am so sore, I think my arms, legs, and back are going to look for employment elsewhere," I said. "Of course, I am about ready to fire them anyway because they are whiny and not working too well."

Suddenly, Emily went silent and just stared at me, so after a moment, I said, "Other than that, I'm all right."

Emily turned and handed the phone back to her mother. "Grandpa talks funny," she said, "but I still like him."

I'm glad my grandchildren like me, strangeness and all.

Road Closure

Our small university town is undergoing some major road renovations. There are three main exits from the highway into the town, and for some reason, all three were scheduled for work simultaneously.

The work is definitely needed. One of the off-ramps is right near the high school and is also a main connection to the university. At around eight o'clock in the morning, that off-ramp backs up for miles on the freeway.

The second off-ramp is the one into the center of town. It becomes a secondary flow for traffic when the first one is backed up. At around eight in the morning and close to five in the afternoon, it comes to a near standstill.

The third off-ramp has extensive construction going on around it and is also the main thoroughfare for those going to the local Walmart. Everything is reduced to twenty-five miles an hour, but don't plan on going that speed. Around four in the afternoon, it comes to a complete stop.

When I need to travel at the peak times, I turn on my GPS, which routes me out of town on a small country road to the next small town. But apparently, others are getting the same information as I am, because there is a line of cars following that route.

To help things out initially, stoplights were installed at the second interchange. Those worked amazingly well, and some people suggested they should just do that at all the off-ramps. Apparently, that solution was too easy. Instead, they are completely tearing things up and doing major renovations.

I was talking to a friend about it. Ted lives in another small town. That town only has a single ramp off the highway. If it is shut down, the only way in or out of town is to follow a narrow road for miles to where it connects to the state highway.

I knew they had endured significant construction last year, and I asked Ted how it went.

He smiled. "Before the construction started, everyone complained about all the problems with getting off at that off-ramp, but it was nothing compared to having it closed. For months we dealt with the challenge of going around. It was a big day when they finally opened it back up."

"Was it better?" I asked.

This time, he laughed. "Better than what? Better than when they started?" He shook his head. "I don't think they really did anything different from what was there before. They may have widened it a bit and put in curbing, but there was no difference in the traffic flow."

"I bet everyone was upset about that," I said.

He shook his head. "On the contrary. Have you ever heard the story of the man and his wife who complained to an old sage that their home was too small? He told them to bring the cow inside. They tried it for a week and said it didn't help. He also told them to bring in the horse. Again, they tried it for a week and said it didn't help. He kept having them add more animals until they couldn't move. He then told them to put all the animals out. Suddenly, they found their home was roomy, and they were happy."

"So, the construction was like that?" I asked.

He nodded. "After how miserable it was trying to get anywhere during the construction, even though they really didn't do anything, it seemed like it was so much better when they finished. Everyone was happy and complimented them on a job well done."

I laughed. "Maybe that's why they decided to do all three exits in our town at the same time. Everyone will probably feel it is a wonderful job when it's done, no matter what they do."

"It's always a possibility," Ted said, "and likely happens more often than we think."

The Loyal Dog

✦

I was working in my yard when a van stopped on the road in front of our house. It's not unusual for cars to stop there and use our driveway to turn around. The house numbering on our street is strange. Not only do addresses switch from east to west in the middle between the two end roads, but the even and odd numbers switch sides of the road. Our address is the best-marked one, and we have a big driveway, so it makes a good turnaround spot.

But this van was different. I only glanced up when they stopped and then went about my work, but then the van sped away quickly when it left. That caused me to look up, and when I did, I saw a dog standing there.

It's common for people to drop their unwanted pets off in the country for others to deal with them. We have had it happen many times. We have often tried to take care of the animals and worked to find a loving home for them. A few times, we have adopted the animals ourselves, but we couldn't afford to do that for all of them.

This dog looked like it was mostly an Australian Shepherd. It looked confused and lost, and I wondered what it would do.

It was midmorning when the dog was dropped off, and it just lay down on the edge of the road, seemingly waiting for its owner to return. The dog was on the road far enough that cars had to move over to miss it. Each time one came, it would get up and stare intently at the vehicle as if looking to see if its owner was among those in it. But the sad thing was, I knew the owner had no intention of returning.

As it got to be evening, I thought the dog might be hungry. I thought I would take it some food, but I didn't get within thirty yards of it before it ran away. Others stopped and also tried to feed it or coax it to their home where they could help it, but it was only looking for those it knew and always ran off.

Someone called an animal shelter, and two of the staff tried to catch the dog, but it ran away and disappeared across the edge of the pasture a couple hundred yards away. But shortly after they left, it was back lying in the same spot, waiting for the people it knew.

My wife posted online about the dog, hoping the owner would know how much they were missed and would feel guilty. Instead, more people came, trying to help, only to have the dog run away. As days went by, I worried about it. I knew it had to be hungry. I also thought about how it responded to everyone. As much as it feared people, I doubted it was treated kindly at home, yet it was still loyal to those it knew and loved.

Eventually, a county animal control officer came and tranquilized the dog. It was taken to a shelter and fed. It started to trust people a little and was eventually put up for adoption. Its story had become widely known because of online posts, and a nice family, with children excited to love it, took it home. But it didn't stay long, and the family soon posted online that the dog was missing.

Looking out on the road by our property, I saw it was back in its place, waiting for its original owners. I just watched it because I didn't want to post about it and have half the county back again. I thought I'd try to directly message the family about the dog if it stayed too long. But after an hour or two, the dog disappeared without anyone chasing it away. The family then let everyone know the dog had returned.

It never ran away from them again. Maybe it wanted to give its previous owner one last chance, but it finally realized that they were never coming back. Perhaps it sensed it had an opportunity to love another family and be loved in return.

And I was happy to know that the dog's deep loyalty could now be trusted to those who would honor it.

My Dad at My Age

I had just hooked the hay conveyer on the side of the truck and climbed on the back. My mother was driving.

"Make sure you have it in third gear, high axle," I called to her. "I would like to have at least two bales always coming up."

My Mom leaned out the window. "This isn't a contest, son."

"Yes, it is," I replied.

"Who are you competing against?" she asked.

"Myself and my best time," I said. "My best time is just under twenty-four minutes, and I want to get it under twenty."

In all reality, I knew I wasn't just competing against myself. I was competing against all my brothers who had gone before me. Of the seven boys in my family, I was next to youngest. I was always relegated to menial hay-hauling jobs because of my age. But now, most of my older brothers were married or off to college, and it was my time to show what I could do.

Our truck hauled around 220 bales, and my brothers talked of loading it in less than thirty minutes. I was sixteen, in good shape, and had made a personal goal to not only beat their record but to beat it by a lot. My mom started the truck, and I checked my watch.

Mom tried to keep the bales coming as fast as she could, but there was always turnaround time at the end of the field. I kept the bales moving off the conveyor and onto the truck, and there was never a pileup. When I called out that it was the last bale, Mom stopped the truck. I threw the bale into place and checked my time, just under twenty-two minutes.

I sighed in disappointment, even though I had beat my best time by two minutes. Mom also checked the time, saw how fast I had loaded the truck, and told me she felt I was crazy and was going to have a heart attack.

I then aimed for my second challenge: getting six loads each day. That was hard, especially with the driving distance, but my brothers had done it. I didn't aim to better them on that because I often had to unload alone and felt that just matching their number was a lofty goal.

When I pulled in to unload, I jumped out and started throwing bales off the truck onto the stack. I would usually throw a couple of layers onto the highest level, then climb down and move the truck forward. With a couple of layers gone, I was lower and would have to throw the bales upward again, but onto a lower level. By gradually moving forward to various levels, I could empty the truck, then get up on the stack and stack all the bales at once. I soon finished and was ready to go.

That evening, I pulled in the last truck to unload shortly before dark. I had to unload it to have it count for matching my brothers, so I started to work. My father came out to help me. Even though I was throwing bales above my waist onto the stack, I quickly had too many for him to keep ahead of me. I finished unloading the truck and stacked more than half of the load.

I remember thinking at that time about the many stories my dad told about how hard and long he had worked when he was young, and I felt doubtful his younger self could have kept up with me. My skepticism was compounded the day I loaded the truck in less than twenty minutes. The conditions worked out almost perfectly with mile-long rows and short turnarounds. I was also getting six loads every day. So, the day I reached my goal, I felt especially invincible.

As Father's Day rolled around this last week, I was thinking about that summer. I realized that when I was sixteen, my father was exactly the age I am now. I thought not of the work I did back then, but of the work he did, and I was amazed at what he was able to do. Being in my sixties, I find my energy level lower, my strength diminished, and my endurance almost nonexistent. Yet my father, even though he worked slower than me, had worked steadily and continually until the job was done.

I thought about what a great father I had. But mostly, I thought about all he taught me and how much I miss him.

In the Doghouse

Rod was not the best at skilled jobs that required him to work with his hands. Even simple things like his son's Klondike Derby car ended up looking like a piece of wood chewed by a beaver with wheels attached. And it didn't run any better than it looked. So, with his history in building things, the family all looked skeptical the day he announced he was building a house for their new dog.

"But, Honey," his wife said, "you have never built anything that complicated. Why don't you just buy one?"

"I'm just building a doghouse, not a mansion," he laughed. "How hard can it be? And have you looked at the ridiculous price of a store-bought one? I can build it myself for half of that."

His oldest son rolled his eyes. "Why don't we just let the dog live in the house? It would be easier."

"First off," Rod said, "I grew up on a farm and learned that all animals belong outside. I'm already annoyed at having the dog sleep in the garage until I get his house built. Second, a dog tends to stink up things. And third, I don't want the dog getting pampered. We let it in the house, and the next thing you know, it will think it has to sleep on my bed."

No one could talk Rod out of it, and when he came home with a load of lumber the following Saturday, the family resigned themselves to the fact that there would be a doghouse. But when Rod asked if anyone wanted to join in the fun, he had no takers.

"When it is finished, knowing how Dad builds things, I don't want anyone thinking I had anything to do with it," the oldest daughter said.

"Well then, I'll just claim all the credit when it turns out beautifully," Rod said.

"You can count on it," his daughter replied.

Rod got at it. He had in mind what he wanted it to look like. He cut one board just more than four feet. The rest of the board was close to the same, so he used it for the opposing corner. Surely it wouldn't matter if it were an inch or two different. He faced the same issue many times, making the same decision. He was proud of his frugality. It was late afternoon when he finished it, and he called the family out to view his work.

Everyone gathered and stared at it. "Is it supposed to lean to one corner like that?" Rod's wife asked.

"It will make the water and snow roll off the roof better," Rod replied.

The family stood there, not knowing what to say, when a friend of Rod's stopped by. Rod brought him over to where the family was. "What do you think of our new doghouse?"

The friend stared at it momentarily, then said, "That is the ugliest thing I have ever seen. I hope you didn't pay good money for it. If you did, you should take it back and get a refund."

The family members' snickering and glancing at Rod must have clued the friend in that Rod built it because he suddenly got a mortified look and said, "Of course, all that really matters is what the dog thinks of it."

They called the dog over, and he seemed thrilled at the attention. But when he was pushed up to the doghouse, he sniffed it, then backed away. When Rod tried to push him into it, he growled, wiggled free, ran, and hid.

The friend laughed. "Maybe it will grow on him. No other dog will have one quite like it."

And that's how the dog ended up sleeping on Rod's bed. As for the doghouse, Rod invited his family to join him for a wiener roast when he burned it. And everyone complimented him on his ability to make a good fire.

Fulfilling a Dream

As I considered the Fourth of July holiday, I thought back to my teenage years. When I was fourteen, there was a National Scout Jamboree, and the group from Idaho had an itinerary to visit many historical sites related to our country's founding and freedoms.

I hadn't heard about the Jamboree until it was past the application deadline, but I decided to apply anyway. I scraped together all the money I had saved and sent in my application. I was accepted, but only as an alternate. No one dropped out, but there ended up being an extra seat on the bus, so I was allowed to go.

As an alternate, I especially had some magnificent adventures that would be worth telling another day, but one of the things I was most excited about was going to the Statue of Liberty. I had dreamed about that for years.

After the Jamboree ended, we headed up the coast, visiting Independence Hall, Gettysburg, and many other historical sites. But I can remember well the day we visited the Statue of Liberty. We stayed on army bases during our travels, and they fed us breakfast for a dollar. We were told to eat well, because it would be a long time before we could get lunch.

I can remember climbing aboard the ferry and the thrill I felt with the beauty of the harbor before us. I stayed right at the forward rail as we traveled to Liberty Island. The spray from the water splashed into my face and felt refreshing in the August heat. I watched as the statue gradually grew bigger as we moved closer. My excitement increased until I could hardly contain it. Finally, we pulled up at the dock, but before we could debark, our head leader made an announcement.

"We have a full day here in New York," he said. "The chance of you getting clear up to the room inside the statue crown before we leave will be unlikely, because we have to return to the mainland for lunch. I suggest you spend your time doing other things."

I could feel the disappointment wash over me. It was disappointing to make it all the way here and not get to go up inside the statue. As we walked ashore, the group of scouts I was with visited about it.

"Howard, what are you going to do?" one asked.

"I'm going to try to make the climb," I replied.

"But you just heard what our leader said," another scout said.

"He said we likely wouldn't have time," I replied. "He didn't say it was an absolute impossibility. I've got to try."

We debated it amongst ourselves. Two other scouts agreed with me, but the others told us we would waste our time standing in line for nothing. Our group split up, with the two scouts going with me, and the others heading off to the little souvenir shop.

The three of us climbed the stairs to the end of the line waiting to get into the room in the statue crown. The line moved slowly, and just about the time we knew we were getting close, our scout leaders passed word up the line that we had to catch the next ferry and needed to turn back, or we would get left behind. The three of us expressed our disappointment, and were turning around, when the man in front of us in line turned to us.

"I don't think you need to worry about being left," he said. "They aren't going anywhere without me."

It was then that we realized he was the bus driver. "I didn't come all the way here just to miss this," he said. "We may miss lunch with them, but we'll have our own."

We continued on up, and I enjoyed realizing one of my greatest wish list items. When we got down, the ferry had just pulled out, and the others were mocking us from their place on the boat. We ate there on the island, and when we got back to the mainland, the others had finished lunch and were waiting at the bus. They were annoyed that the bus driver was with us and told us about the fancy lunch we missed.

Fulfilling a dream was worth missing a fancy lunch.

Garage Sales

My wife, Donna, likes to go to garage sales. Now and then she'll take a Saturday morning and enjoy the treasure hunt. Sometimes she comes home with next to nothing, and sometimes she comes home with some prize. Now that we are grandparents, she usually comes home with things for the grandchildren.

I'm not much of a person for garage sales. Even when I go shopping, I usually have one or two things in mind to get, and I get them and get out. But at garage sales, you have to wander through a lot of things you don't need to occasionally find one thing you do.

One Sunday, Donna was visiting with her friend, Ann, and the subject of garage sales came up.

"I love to go to them," Donna said. "Daris goes with me occasionally, but he isn't much of one to wander around and buy anything."

Ann laughed. "My husband is just the opposite. I try not to let him know I plan to go, because if I do, he will go along, and, frankly, we can't afford it."

"What do you mean?" Donna asked.

"If Brian knows I'm going, he will peruse the ads online and in the newspaper. He figures out which ones have the things he would like the most, and then he puts them in order of priority. We start early in the morning and follow his planned route."

"So, the problem is, you want to go to other ones or go alone?" Donna asked.

Ann shook her head. "Not really. I like his company, and I just write down the addresses and soon forget what they're selling, so I don't care which ones we go to or the order."

"Does he spend too much money?" Donna asked.

Again, Ann shook her head. "It isn't even that. He is the king of bargaining. It's what he buys."

"How's that?" Donna asked.

"Let me give you an example," Ann said. "One day, he planned our day to start at an estate sale. An old couple was selling their property after living there for fifty years, and they had a lot of stuff they needed to clear out before they could list it. The husband had become incapacitated, so the wife was running the sale.

"While Brian headed for the detached garage, I wandered through the house. I found a few things I could use, but most of what they had were older versions of new items I had that were more efficient. I admit that I was tempted to buy a few things that worked by hand and didn't need electricity, but I couldn't think where I would put them in my kitchen.

"Eventually, I made my way out to the garage. To my surprise, Brian had his pickup backed up to the door, and the back was piled high above the cab, mostly with woodworking equipment. I gasped and asked him what he was doing. Before he could answer, the sweet little lady said, 'All is okay here, dear. You just go back to the house.' She held my hand and led me back to the house before returning to the garage.

"Brian soon was strapping things down, preparing to leave. As he climbed into the pickup, he turned to the lady and said, 'I'll be back over the next few days to finish hauling everything.' I was shocked and asked how much he bought. He said the lady wanted the garage cleared so they had bargained a price for a few hundred dollars for him to take it all."

Ann shook her head and sighed. "I asked him where he planned to put it, and he said he'd been planning to add on to his shop."

Ann looked at Donna and smiled. "That's why I can't afford to take him garage saling with me."

The Bread Machine

Before I left home, I had my mother teach me to cook the things I liked, especially homemade bread. When Donna and I were dating, I did most of the cooking. I had been living on my own for some time and had become a good cook. Donna's mother, on the other hand, wouldn't let anyone in her kitchen when she prepared food, so neither Donna nor her siblings had learned to cook.

When we got engaged, Donna did a lot more cooking and had a natural talent for it. Her bread soon rivaled mine. There was only one time it turned out badly, and that was when my mother stopped by and decided to help. They say that too many cooks spoil the broth. I don't know about the broth, but I do know that what they made together was less than desirable.

For many years, Donna made bread for our large family and taught all of our children to as well. But our lives started to change as our last children headed off to school. Donna took on other activities, teaching and working on music, and her life was extremely busy. It was hard for her to find the time for many things, bread baking included. That was when I suggested she get a bread machine.

She knew it wasn't an insult to her cooking, but it was still hard for her to think she didn't have time for those things that were so important as our children were growing up. I told her she could just stick in the ingredients she always had and leave it to the machine to do all the mixing and baking. She said she would think about it.

The next day, she called me at work. "The strangest thing happened today. You know our friend, Grace? Well, she called today and asked if I could use a bread machine. Isn't that a strange coincidence?"

I laughed. "Extremely."

"You didn't tell anyone we were thinking about getting one, did you?" Donna asked.

"No. I felt the decision had to be yours."

"Well, I decided it wouldn't hurt to try it," she said. "Could you pick it up after work?"

I assured her I would, and when I finished, I went to Grace's house. She was a bit older than we were, and her children had left home.

When I knocked, Grace answered the door. She told me the machine was in the garage and led me to the side of the house. She pushed the buttons on the pad and opened the big door. There was the bread machine sitting prominently in the front of the car slot. It looked like it had hardly been used.

"Did you decide to quit making bread since your children are all gone?" I asked.

Grace shook her head. "You can't quit doing something that you never started."

That surprised me. I knew Grace was a good cook and just assumed she made homemade bread.

She must have seen my surprise, because she laughed. "It's not that I didn't try to make bread now and then. My children had homemade bread at neighbors' and friends' houses, and they wanted us to make it, too. But that was one thing I could never master. The bread always turned out like a brick off an ancient pyramid. After a few attempts, the children wouldn't ask again for about a year, and then the process would repeat itself."

"So, where does the bread machine fit into this?" I asked.

"For Mother's Day this year, my children decided to help me out and all chipped in to buy it for me."

"Did that help?" I asked.

She shook her head. "For some of us, it just means we can make bad bread faster and easier."

I laughed as I picked up the little machine. The bread Donna made with it was always good, and after talking to Grace, I was grateful.

Motorcycle Accident and Chaos

There is a saying that goes, "If you want something done right, ask the busiest person." Kaylyn thought about that when she was asked to head the fundraiser for the little charter school that her children attended. With her husband, Jack, on the city council, she bore most of the responsibility for their three children, and she doubted anyone could be busier than she was. Still, she accepted.

As things often happen, everything hit at once. On the weekend of the fundraiser, the mayor, Jack, and the rest of the city council had a meeting with the governor. She was grateful that the ladies she had asked to help pulled through on their assignments, and the fundraiser went well. The event brought in even more than expected, money that the little school desperately needed.

Kaylyn was also grateful that her oldest had reached the age where she could care for things at home and watch the two younger children. Because there was over ten thousand dollars, Kaylyn wanted to finish things up and get the money to the bank, so she sent her children home with a friend. She had already prepared for this and had their favorite snacks and the movie they wanted.

After everyone else was gone, Kaylyn had to count the money to record it on the form that would go with the deposit envelope that she would have to put in the drop box since the bank was closed. She had piled most of the quarters, dimes, nickels, and multiple denominations of bills into piles set out all over the school office floor when her cell phone rang. It was her oldest daughter, and Kaylyn had forgotten to send the house key with them, leaving her children locked out of the house.

Kaylyn hated leaving that much money just sitting on the school floor, but she quickly locked up and rushed home. She had just opened the door for her children when she saw the motorcycle. Jack had been teaching her to ride it and encouraged her to do so when she drove alone. "The van takes a lot of gas," he told her. "And the motorcycle will save money." She decided to take it. She knew it would please Jack to know she was trying to conserve their family finances.

Kaylyn had only reached the first intersection from their home when she had trouble. A dump truck had spilled some sand there, and when she hit it, the motorcycle started to slide. Trying to keep balance, she laid the motorcycle almost flat as she slid across the intersection and onto the median. She was banged up a fair amount, and her leg was swollen, but all she could think about was the money that she was responsible for sitting on the school floor.

She knew the motorcycle wasn't going anywhere, so she left it there and limped home as quickly as she could. She told her children what she was doing, then rushed off in the van to return to the school.

It wasn't long before the police found the abandoned motorcycle. They traced the plate and went to Kaylyn's home. When they asked the children if they knew anything about why the motorcycle had been left in the middle of the road, the oldest daughter told them that her mother said she had to rush back to get the money that had been left on the ground.

And that was when the real trouble began. The police had just dealt with some major drug busts, and an abandoned vehicle and money all over the ground sounded like a hot case, if ever there was one. They asked to search the house, and the children invited them in. Not finding anything besides the regular laundry and other housework to be done, they decided to look deeper, and that's when the trail led to Jack, who was involved in the conversation at the governor's office. Meanwhile, Kaylyn was innocently counting the school's money, not knowing that Jack, the police, and the governor's office were now all on high alert, looking for her.

(To be continued)

Motorcycle Accident and Chaos
(part 2)

✦

    Kaylyn was in charge of the charter school fundraiser. It raised more than ten thousand dollars, and afterward, she sent her children home with a friend so she could get the money in the bank. But she had barely laid out the money into piles on the floor to count it when her daughter called and needed her to come to unlock the house since she forgot to send a key. After opening the house, she decided to take the motorcycle to save money but wrecked it just down the street from her house. She limped home, got the van, and hurried to get the money safely in the bank.

    The problem was, the police found the abandoned motorcycle, and after running a check, they went to her house. The children said their mom was busy counting a lot of money that was on the ground, and the police immediately suspected drug dealing. Jack, Kaylyn's husband, was on the city council and was away with the rest of the council and the mayor to a meeting with the governor. The police searched the house, and being unable to contact Kaylyn, whose phone was broken in the crash, they contacted Jack.

    As the police talked to Jack, they heard the mayor speaking in the background. They then called the mayor and informed him they thought a big drug deal had gone down, and it sounded like Jack's wife was involved. This aroused the governor's curiosity, and by the time Kaylyn dropped the money off at the bank, the police, Jack, the mayor, and even the governor's state troopers were searching for her.

    Happy to have the fundraiser done, Kaylyn headed home, feeling great satisfaction in her accomplishment, ignoring the bruises and bit of bleeding from the wreck. But when she turned the corner onto her street, she saw police cars with lights flashing surrounding the motorcycle. Looking beyond them, she could see more surrounding her house. She couldn't believe they were making such a big deal of an abandoned vehicle. They usually gave a person a couple of days to retrieve it.

She stopped by the police cars, and the police chief immediately recognized her. He ordered her out of the vehicle in such a commanding voice that it surprised her.

"Where have you been?" he demanded.

"Just taking care of money," Kaylyn replied.

"Uh, huh," he said. "And just how much was it?"

"Over ten thousand dollars," Kaylyn replied, proud they had made so much.

The police chief nodded as if everything was coming together as they expected. "And how did you get the bruises and the gashes?"

Kaylyn pointed at the motorcycle. "I wrecked the bike."

"Were you speeding to get to the money?" the chief asked.

"Not much," Kaylyn replied.

"I think you are going to have to come with us to the station," the chief said.

At this, Kaylyn began to cry. "But I have children at home. Isn't this a lot over just abandoning a vehicle?"

"It's a lot bigger than that," the chief said.

By this time, a newspaper reporter was there, and Kaylyn was growing more confused by the minute. The mayor talked to the police and pressed them to make sure the newspaper and community knew they were cracking down on crime. Jack finally was able to speak to Kaylyn, and she sobbed that she was sorry about the motorcycle and didn't understand why the police were making such a big deal of it.

When Jack explained that the police thought it all had to do with drugs, Kaylyn began to understand how it all appeared. Through her tears, she haltingly explained about the fundraiser. The police chief verified where the money was from, and finally, everything settled down. The police even helped her get the motorcycle home.

But Kaylyn was left with some concerns, since the newspaper reporter left saying there still had to be a story somewhere in the fact that a city council member's wife was almost arrested for drug dealing.

(To be continued)

Motorcycle Accident and Chaos
(Conclusion)

Kaylyn's motorcycle accident, the fact she was depositing a considerable sum of money in the bank, and other circumstances led the police to believe there was a drug bust to be done. By the time it was sorted out, Kaylyn was in tears, and a newspaper reporter was wondering how she could make a story out of a city council member's wife almost being arrested as part of a mistaken drug bust.

The newspaper reporter called soon after Kaylyn's husband, Jack, returned from a meeting the city council and mayor had with the governor.

"I'd like to do a story about your near-arrest experience," she told Kaylyn in a humorous tone.

Kaylyn was so frustrated that she handed the phone to Jack. He talked to the reporter for a while, then hung up and sat down to visit with Kaylyn.

"I don't want anything to do with talking to the reporter, or the police, or anyone mentioning anything to do with that experience ever again," Kaylyn said.

"But, Honey," Jack said, "if there's one thing I have learned from my small foray into politics, it is that if a story is going to be told, it is better to get your side of it out first. I have no doubt that the reporter will write a story one way or another. It would be better if she heard our side of it. Besides, maybe we can turn it into something humorous and positive."

Kaylyn reluctantly agreed that Jack was right, so they set a time for the reporter to visit them. When she came, the family was all nicely dressed. The reporter wanted first to take a picture of the whole family. Then, there was a picture of the wrecked motorcycle. Afterward, they sat down to talk.

Kaylyn shared her part of the story, how she was trying to get the money from the school fundraiser to the bank, how she had wrecked on the motorcycle, and then how confused she was when the police were making such a big deal of what she thought was just an abandoned vehicle case.

Jack talked about being in the meeting with the governor when the police called about the wrecked motorcycle. He was concerned about his wife, but then the conversation turned to information they had that Kaylyn had a large sum of money, and they thought it might be a possible drug situation. He told the police his wife was a good wife and mother and would not have anything to do with drugs.

Jack went on to tell how the police called the mayor and how everything was dissolving into chaos in the governor's office. Then Kaylyn told her about Jack's call and how, after he informed her what the police were thinking, they were trying to get everything straightened out.

Though the reporter found the story funny, Kaylyn still struggled to see the humor. But when the story appeared in the paper, she did have to admit that if she stepped back from the experience and looked at it, it was funny. She just hoped that would be the end of it.

But it wasn't. At a big community gathering, the mayor came up to Kaylyn and apologized for the police thinking she was involved in drugs. Before he finished, there was a small crowd gathered around. Then, one day, when she had some important ladies visiting who were part of a committee she wanted to join, the police knocked at her door. The police chief had sent some flowers, and the police officers apologized profusely for the misunderstanding about her being part of a drug deal. After they left, the ladies stared at Kaylyn, and she eventually had to tell the story.

The ladies laughed, and Kaylyn got to be on the committee. Finally, things began to settle down, and the stares went away. Life was back to boring normal, and Kaylyn was glad.

But she decided that her motorcycling days were over.

If you enjoyed this book, please leave a review on Amazon at: https://www.amazon.com/dp/1629860379

Would you like to see the Life's Outtakes column running in your local paper or magazine? Suggest it to the editor. If an editor runs the Life's Outtakes column due to your suggestion, we will send you a free autographed book by Daris Howard. Feel free to contact us at http://www.publishinginspiration.com

Also, read stories, purchase books, or subscribe to our short story list by going to http://www.publishinginspiration.com

Daris Howard's Amazon page:

http://amzn.com/e/B004reH76UGK

Also, for inspiring plays and books, as well as discounts for booksellers, go to http://www.publishinginspiration.com

About the Author

Daris Howard, an award-winning author and playwright, grew up on an Idaho farm. He was a state champion athlete, competed in college athletics, and lived for a time in New York.

Daris has worked as a cowboy, as a mechanic, in farming, and in the timber industry. He is now a college professor. He has also been a scoutmaster, having up to eighteen boys in his scout troop at a time. In his wide range of experience, he has associated with many colorful characters who form a basis for his writing. Daris has had plays translated into German and French, and his plays have been performed in many countries around the world. For many years, Daris has written the popular column Life's Outtakes, which consists of weekly short stories and is published in various newspapers and magazines in the US and Canada.

www.ingramcontent.com/pod-product-compliance
Lightning Source LLC
Chambersburg PA
CBHW052006220626
47052CB00004B/1114